Ordinary Guy

Ordinary Guy

Book One of the Ordinary Project

Kevin Virgil Wallace

Writers Club Press
San Jose New York Lincoln Shanghai

Ordinary Guy
Book One of the Ordinary Project

Writers Club Press
an imprint of iUniverse.com, Inc.

For information address:
iUniverse.com, Inc.
620 North 48th Street, Suite 201
Lincoln, NE 68504-3467
www.iuniverse.com

ISBN: 0-595-12264-7

Printed in the United States of America

For Brandon

"Some circumstantial evidence is very strong, as when you find a trout in the milk."

—Henry David Thoreau

Foreword

Ordinary Guy is part of a much larger work, which I refer to as *The Ordinary Project*. At this point, it consists of two sequels and a number of poems, songs and works of art, representing two decades of work. *Ordinary Guy* is where the story begins and where the characters are introduced.

When asked what *Ordinary Guy* is about, I've always had difficulty answering. To me it is ultimately about the interconnectedness of all things. I suppose that it could be seen as an adventure and love story.

A number of people assisted with The Ordinary Project. When someone would say "You're writing a book—I'd like to read it", I took that to mean that they would assist in editing it. I owe a special thanks to Robert Christy who read an early draft and offered very good advice and how it might be turned into something which made some amount of sense. Kirsten Muenster read and edited all three books in the series and was of great assistance.

None of my writing would have gotten so far without the love and patience of my wife Sheryl. I wish that everyone had the pleasure of a mate who accepts them for what they are, allowing them to do their work, rather than seeking to change them into something they're not. It is a wonderful gift, fo4r which I am eternally grateful.

Prelude

"Okay, how's this…It begins with music. You are walking down the trail from your treehouse, as your theme song plays…"

"C'mon, Randy…I was upset when you died, but you know, I figured it at least meant that idea of yours would get a rest…"

"No, that's the good thing about writing songs…it gives you some amount of immortality."

"Yeah, I suppose."

"So, how are you planning on starting off?" He was apparently quite interested in the project.

"In the middle."

"Why's that?"

"Well, I was thinking…it seems to me that most people who read the book will be in the midst of their own stories, so I would drop them into the middle of mine."

"And what song will be playing?"

"I don't know. I hadn't thought about it. I didn't figure that it mattered."

Brad knew as he said it that he shouldn't have. That Randy felt differently.

"Of course it does…it could be a musical. You realize that the Hollywood musical is going to make a come back, don't you?"

"Oh, not that idea of a musical…"

"Listen, let me work on the project with you."

Brad never thought it right to remind Randy that he was dead and so it was difficult for him to explain why this wouldn't be feasible.

"We'll see." Brad said.

A Voodoo Ceremony

The locals all came for the ceremony. Everyone knew that the Snakespirit clan always put on a great party and that there would be food and drink for all. Aside from this, there was the usual attraction of voodoo dancing, scantily clad bodies and an element of danger.

A small mid-western family had been invited. They were staying at a local bed and breakfast, and having heard about the ceremony, decided that it would be a good cultural experience. Perhaps it would give the boys something to tell about in their "how I spent my summer vacation" reports at school.

Everyone gathered in a clearing in the forest, surrounded by large, misshapen trees. It was a hot, humid night, and everyone wore the the minimum of clothing and kept drinks in their hands. Father fell into the spirit of things very easily. It seemed to be a night like no other, and this was a new and different world. As the drummers played, the women danced, and the boys watched, in awe. One of the dancers often swooped over in front of them, shaking her body, and pulling at the older boy's hair. Mother was having trouble feeling comfortable with all of this, suspecting that it was not fitting entertainment for a good Catholic family.

"I'm going to get another beer." Father said, climbing to his feet.

"Oh...okay." Mother said, her hesitation and reservation evident, though ignored. "But hurry back."

Passing a large tent, he noticed an attractive woman dancing alone near the entrance. It seemed to him that she was wearing a great deal of jewelry, and practically no clothing.

"They certainly don't have women like that back in Bay Springs." He thought to himself.

She noticed him as well and her eyes were suddenly locked upon his. She continued her dance. He thought for a moment about the head of John the Baptist, then walked slowly toward her. She smiled and, as he neared, she slipped into the tent. Without hesitation or reservation, he followed her.

She was standing there, smiling at him.

"Uh, hello..." He stammered.

She just stood there, looking into his eyes, smiling and beginning to move her body again. This time she danced very slowly.

"Sure is an exciting ceremony." He said, trying to make conversation.

"Yes." She said. "It's a special ceremony for my son."

"Oh, you have a family?...And a husband." He glanced about nervously, worried that it was a trap of some sort. If it wasn't, it would certainly be a compromising situation for her husband to find them in.

"Had a husband...have a son." She explained. "He's thirteen. You have sons yourself, don't you?..."

"Yes...my middle boy is the same age as yours."

"Isn't that a coincidence?" She moved closer to him, pressing her body against his.

"Why are they having a party for him?..." He continued his attempt to make conversation, but she kissed him, causing the conversation to segue into something else, which he found very pleasurable.

Going Home

Brad drove down the Louisiana highway, having gone through quite a bit for an ordinary guy.

His father, Lenny Mitchell, was riding in the backseat. Brad was angry with him and yet sure that his father was at least a bit ashamed. Lenny knew that Brad expected a better explanation of how all this could come to be and was trying to find a way to put it into words.

Beside Brad sat the girl he would spend the rest of his life with. Having fallen in love, a sense of unknowing can gnaw at one's heart. Brad knew through prophecy that this relationship would pan out. As she smiled at him and squeezed his hand, he felt good about it all. Admittedly, it was disturbing to consider that within a few days he would be digging up the decayed bodies of her great Uncle and his friends. It meant a great deal to her and she'd certainly done almost as much for him in Louisiana. Brad knew that he would be able to deal with it.

"When Wanda was younger she looked like Cleopatra." Lenny said.

Brad looked at him in the rear view mirror. He was sure his father sensed that he wasn't as interested in the relationship with Wanda, as he was the betrayal of his mother. Lenny thought for a moment, then started to explain it from a different angle.

"I used to be an altar boy and one day Father stood with me before a statue of the Virgin and told me how unworthy we were of her love..." He explained slowly, seeming more honest than Brad had seen him in years. "I had never strayed and I was a good husband...hell, I was even a good Catholic. But then, after that night with Wanda, I felt so unworthy of your mother and I suppose that I placed her on that same pedestal that Father and I had stood before that day."

Brad nodded his head, to say that he didn't need to hear anymore. Whether he believed what his father was saying, or if he didn't want to hear it, wasn't apparent to either of them. Lenny didn't explain any further. Brad was a grown man and had to accept all that he had learned about his father and about his own life. He was in love and it was best to concentrate upon the positive aspects of his changed life.

Growing Up

Brad's life in the North Woods had been sheltered, yet filled with rare experience. He had always reacted to the abnormal aspects by being less conspicuous in his behavior and by remaining on the family homestead, in his home town. For every way that Brad was unusual, he counteracted with extreme normality in another aspect of his life. He supposed, in retrospect, that he confused normality with his need to seem an ordinary guy.

When Brad was a child, he built a tree house. It was his idea, but his brothers wholeheartedly agreed and convinced their father to assist them. As the years went by, the treehouse grew, although his brothers had lost interest and it became Brad's sole responsibility. A stairway took the place of the ladder and soon a ground level was started. He continued to work on the place until it became a cottage and his home.

Approaching his mid-thirties, Brad supposed that it was a little odd that he'd never been in love. He'd had some social and sexual experience, but his heart had never been brave enough to consider taking in another. For this reason he had always been something of a loner. Since graduation from high school, his life had changed very little, aside from becoming less active.

The North Woods had always been his home. He slept and ate in the home of his parents during most of his youth, yet his experiences, from playing with friends as a child to adolescent exploits, had been centered in the woods. As an adult, this continued to be the case.

The woods stretched from Brad's parent's house for miles back into state land. There were places within them, castaway or deserted, which became sacred to his life.

A large boulder that jutted out over a bluff and offered a wonderful view was one of these places. It was called The Edge. For kids it was part of an initiation, to go all the way out to the very edge of the boulder. There they proved their bravery, taking in a near death experience. As the years passed it was a place to go and sit, alone or with a friend.

There was the field of abandoned cars, where a group of rusted antique vehicles sat, for the most part without engines. It was some distance from the narrowest of dirt roads and no one could say exactly how they came to be there or why. The kids who grew up in the area had broken all of the windows years before. The glass had all been swept out onto the ground, so that they could sit inside the cars. During the day, from The Edge, this place had the strangest appearance. The cars sat there, as if they'd gathered for a meeting, with the sun reflecting on millions of pieces of broken glass.

Building a Home

From the beginning, Brad envisioned a treehouse like no other, although as a boy he hardly imagined that as a man he would call it home. He had chosen the largest tree on the family property. It was set back a half mile from the house and not everyone agreed that this would be best. Brad's little brother wanted the treehouse to be closer to the house, so that he could shout for mother if there were any problem. His older brother, who felt that he'd outgrown the desire for a treehouse, but was going along with the program, didn't want to walk too far to visit it. For him, it would be a place to go off and have a cigarette or a drink and it only needed to be out of sight of their parents. There was also the problem of traveling all that distance, down the trail, with the building materials.

Brad did everything he could to convince his father that his location would indeed be the best. Lenny Mitchell's concern was with safety and he wanted to be sure that the tree they chose would be able to support the structure. He had a friend, an engineer who worked at the power plant, who offered to come and take a look. Brad led his father and the engineer through the woods, to the tree he had chosen. They took a look at the tree, then glanced around at the others.

"It's the oldest, the largest and the strongest." The engineer stated. "Those branches there would make an excellent support. I can do some drawings for you, to show you how to build the structure."

It was decided. It would be Brad's tree. From the beginning, it was a project that he put all of his time and effort into. His vision of what it could be grew as he worked. His brothers interest in the treehouse diminished everyday and by the time they actually had an enclosed room with a ladder leading up to it, the treehouse was considered Brad's place. He continued to work on it over the years and managed to create other small rooms and a stairwell. The year he graduated from high school, he completed a lower level with a living room and fireplace. He decided to attempt living in it full time, despite the fact that it had neither plumbing or electricity.

Knowing that he had all the creature comforts in his parent's house, a half mile down the hill, Brad managed to live there. Winters were difficult. There was no way to heat all of the rooms, so he took to staying on the lower level, sleeping in front of the fireplace. Brad eventually installed pipes and registers and was able to keep the room directly above heated as well. Once he's made it through his first winter, he was very happy. If he'd ever had any doubts, he knew that he had found a way to spend his life in the North Woods. He had a job and a place of his own. He would listen to his battery operated AM radio in the evening, reading and writing by the light of candles and the fireplace.

Waking up, Brad would walk into the woods and piss in the clear quiet morning. He would note the change of the seasons, it all being more apparent, living in a tree. The winters seemed long and silent, but the other seasons would change very quickly and were full of motion and color. Birds and small animals were everywhere, as were his constant enemies, insects. Spiders sought to claim his home and he was constantly placing them outside and destroying their webs. Bees often chose to build their hives in nearby trees and once they had done so, he wasn't able to argue with them. Ants liked him, because he wasn't always good about cleaning up scraps of food, so he was always having to deal with them.

Like every house, Brad's had it's problems and required some maintenance, but he found it to be a wonderful home.

The Painter

Jimmy Snakespirit awoke in his treehouse, set deep in the South Woods. It was just after sunrise and he'd been up late painting. He tried to return to his dream, a rather nice one, about a beautiful girl in a corn field, but was unable to. He decided that he would probably have time to take a long afternoon nap. Sitting on the edge of his bed, he reached out and picked up a small painting on board that was laying on the floor. He studied it for a moment.

"Can't make heads or tails of this one." He said to himself, as he climbed to his feet and went to the door. He hesitated for a moment, as harsh sunlight hit his face, then continued on down the stairs. They were primitive, he'd built them himself and was no master craftsman. He had to watch his step as not to step on a weak board here and there, but they were better than the ladder he'd used as a child.

He started down the hill to the family house, painting in hand. He continued to study it. It was abstract, with some figurative elements, but he couldn't really make out the scene. He thought it a nice painting however, perhaps one of his best.

Grandma was sitting on the porch, watching the road. It seemed that she was always there. Jimmy walked up and handed her the painting. She took a long look at it, her face not changing it's expression.

"It's a bad one." She said, handing it back to him. "You'll have to burn it."

Jimmy took the painting, and started back up the hill. This wasn't criticism, it was judgment and he was accustom to it. Still he liked the painting and studied it again. Back at his treehouse, he slid it under his bed, with several others, without a thought.

The Drive

Brad had given Marcia a tape of songs his friend Randy had recorded in Los Angeles. They had written several of the songs together and Brad wanted her to hear them. Marcia seemed to enjoy the tape and they had listened to it often on their drive south. Being rather analytical and knowing that Brad had written the lyrics, she would often ask about subject matter and meanings. He was somewhat flattered that she thought that the songs were good. He was happy to have the opportunity to tell her about his experiences and consider the way he felt about things.

Brad knew that his father recognized the songs, although he said nothing. Being a musician himself, Lenny Mitchell had been very supportive of Randy and Brad writing songs. Brad suspected that his father had an understanding of Randy's dreams which he'd lacked. Perhaps he had come to think of him as a son, as he was over so often and they'd gotten along so well. The look on his father's face suggested that, listening to the music, they were feeling the same thing…considering things in retrospect and trying to connect it all to their current situation and the future. It was a time of losing people and it was best to deal with that; save some love in one's heart and move on. For better or worse, it was a time of change. Brad and Lenny Mitchell didn't talk much, but had always maintained a line of communication.

Marcia turned the music up.

"I like this one." She said. The song was Old Foster Farm. It was about the Fosters, but was also about the time Brad had spent there, growing up.

The old Foster place was a deserted cabin dating back to the turn of the century. It was the sight of one of the mysteries of the county, on record at the Historical Society. No one knew what became of old man Foster and his wife. They had kept to themselves, so no one knew for certain when they'd disappeared. It was suspected that they were murdered, as no one just moves away and leaves the house furnished and containing all of the family belongings. It could be that they met with a bear or fell to their deaths somehow in the woods. It was always in the back of Brad's mind that he might come upon two skeletons while hiking and solve the mystery.

The Old Foster Place had always been a good place to gather and tell ghost stories when they were kids and they often camped there. As a teenager, Randy and Brad found that it was a good place to take a couple of girls and a twelve pack of beer. Over the years, it remained a place for Brad to go and write, full of memories and mysteries. He knew that he would share this place with Marcia when they got home.

Brad never imagined that he would ever leave his hometown. He had always felt that the woods, roads, buildings and people were as much a part of him as his body, and that he wouldn't be able to exist without them. His friend Randy, on the other hand, was one of those who couldn't wait to graduate high school and leave the home town behind. That was the only difference between them, an aspect of their personalities that disallowed any understanding of the other's motivations.

Brad was always writing; histories and fictions, poems and whatever came to mind. He knew that he could find success and remain at home, live like Thoreau or a modern male Emily Dickinson. Randy on the other hand played guitar and sang. For him success would have to be found in the city, playing gigs and spending time in the recording studio.

Brad wasn't sure why he'd started writing, it was just something that came to him naturally after he started reading. It was the same way with Randy and listening to records; he went out and bought a guitar and started playing. And this is what brought them together, creative pursuits that set them apart and were lacking in most folks in their town.

Randy and Brad often wrote together. He would go through Brad's notebook and take poems or sometimes lines from stories and put them to music. Before long Brad was coming to Randy with full sets of song lyrics and he would match them up with chord progressions.

"Man, you should come to the city with me..." He would say.

"And leave all this behind?" Brad would answer, waving his hands in the air, whether they were in the woods or the bowling alley coffee shop.

Randy never really understood, but he would nod his head, knowing that Brad felt a need to remain in the North Woods. Randy was one of the few who knew about the gift. He saw existence as being very large and life full of magic. Brad's gift wasn't an odd thing; it was evidence of this way of seeing things.

Brad considered that Randy and he appreciated each other more, with the knowledge that they would eventually part company. Randy would go off to the city and only return again for short visits, while Brad would live the rest of his days in his little home town. Brad imagined that most believed the people in their lives would be there forever and that there would always be time to right any wrongs and explain their feelings. He was sure that people would be better to each other, if they were more aware of the partings that would take place in the future. When Randy died, Brad grieved, but he didn't feel that their friendship was ever lacking; that they didn't honestly know each other.

Nights at The Towers

One night at The Towers, Randy and Brad drank a few beers up on the hill with Susan Fisher, who was very attractive and apparently more fond of Randy than Brad. Brad ended up excusing himself and leaving them alone there. She and Randy became lovers that evening, although she later explained that she would have been as interested in Brad that night. She told him all of this a decade and a half later, when she was a waitress at the Lamplighter. Perhaps it was to flatter him and perhaps she was thinking that he might be wanting his turn. He had it set in his mind that Randy was always more of a ladies man then himself and didn't believe her. She certainly could have seduced him in the weeks or months that followed that night on the hill. By the time she shared this information, Brad wasn't really interested in her at all.

The Towers were two miles from Brad's home, set back in the woods on an old dirt road. It had been the place to meet for drinks and hanky panky for generations and perhaps centuries. That's what the Natives said anyway. They were always there at the parties, suggesting that hallucinogens were a sacrament for them and that everyone was partying on a ceremonial ground out of the kindness of their hearts. Brad had known most of the

Natives from the time he was very young and first wandered out to The Towers. He got along pretty well with most of them.

There were two guys, who would become pretty crazy and violent when they drank. They complained constantly about the old Westerns and how they were racist. Calling all of the white students "cowboys" and singling Brad out, they hung him by his feet in a tree one night. He learned his lesson to know when to avoid them and was reassured that most of the Natives were good folks, when two others found him later that night and helped him down.

The Art World

The landlord left, disappointed to have been paid the month back rent he was owed. He had long ago faced the fact that the gallery owner wasn't making enough money to pay the rent. This was not a problem, as he had been approached by a potential tenant who would be paying more money. After all, rents on the Los Angeles Westside had risen dramatically. Now, it would be a problem evicting the gallery owner, with him up to date on his rent. He had never been impressed with the art which hung on the walls and it seemed a ridiculous way to even attempt making a living.

The telephone rang. Carol, the art dealer's sole employee walked over to her desk and answered.

"Hello, this is William Price." Came the voice on the line.

"Just a moment." Carol said. "I'll get him."

He was on a ladder, attempting to hang a large canvas.

"It's William Price." Carol told him.

"Cool." He said, climbing down the ladder and going to the phone. "Hello, Mr. Price. How are you?"

"Very well. And you?"

"Excellent thanks. You got the message that I sold that Jimmy Snakespirit painting that you consigned to me?"

"Yes I did. Congratulations."

"Well thanks, I appreciate the opportunity. It was a great piece and things have been a little slow, so I needed the sale."

"Should we be expecting the check?"

"Yes, of course. I was calling in hopes that you might send another piece or two. I think I can sell more work."

"Well, to be quite honest, demand is high for Jimmy's work and I only have a limited supply. But let me see what I can do..."

William Price hung up the phone and considered that it had not been so long ago that he had discovered Jimmy Snakespirit. He had gone to New Orleans to appraise the collection of a recently deceased matron of the arts, considering it a vacation. He had no interest in escaping the art world, but he thought it would be good to experience different sites, different food and different people. He never had an interest in southern folk art and didn't expect to be put on the trail of a self trained artist while there. In fact, his world was scholarly and there was little room for contemporary primitivism in it. Usually the gallery exhibited art about art and conceptual work.

If you had to ask what it meant, you didn't belong in the gallery and if you had to ask what it cost, you couldn't afford it. It was all about pomposity and intellectual games. The eighties had been very good to the Werner/Price gallery and had supplied capital to insure that they would be around for a very long time.

Mrs. Littleton had a large art collection, which the family hoped to dispose of through the gallery or at auction. There were a number of Nineteenth Century French Paintings, not Price's thing, but worth a fair amount of money. She'd purchased a number of Joseph Cornell boxes early on and had decorated her kitchen with them. Each of these could easily bring five figures. And then there were the four paintings by an artist he had never heard of, named Jimmy Snakespirit. He didn't recognize them as the work of a self taught artist. They appeared to be abstract, but upon closer examination seemed to have narrative aspects to them. They looked a bit like the work that was currently being done in Germany. He spent a great deal of time studying them and realized that they were very good.

When William Price returned, with a group of small paintings under his arm, he had nodded to the receptionist and gone straight back to his partner's office.

"Ah, you're back...good." Thomas Werner looked up from a portfolio at his partner and managed the closest thing to a smile he was capable of. "How was your vacation?"

"I didn't get much rest...I was put on the trail of a remarkable painter the day I arrived and it was a great deal of work locating him and convincing him to sell me his work."

"Sell you his work?...What are you talking about?...Every hot artist in town would give their firstborn to consign work to us and your spending money to acquire work by some unknown?"

"An unknown primitive on top of that." Price added.

"What?"

"His name is Jimmy Snakespirit." Price began to place the paintings on the table in front of him.

"Snakespirit?...What kind of name is that?"

"I'm not sure...I couldn't tell if they were Black, Indian or Gypsy. They talked like Cajuns from South America..."

"They?..."

"Yes there's a whole group of them...they have a small village out in the woods. The women tell fortunes and the men are artists or entertainers..."

"And so other people are aware of this body of work?..." Thomas Werner was studying the paintings carefully. "...Others have bought paintings from him?..."

"Just locals. He's far from being discovered. I mean, this guy has never really been out of the state and he lives in this house he built in the tree behind his family's home…"

"They really are pretty good."

"I know…Anyway this Jimmy Snakespirit's grandmother has what they call a gift of prophecy and she claims that the paintings contain the fates of those who come to possess them. What we have here are what they call good luck paintings. They burn the ones that the grandmother deems bad luck.

"They burn a percentage of the paintings?"

"Yes, and I've got to tell you, I've seen the bad luck paintings and they're even better than these…"

"These are nice paintings…Couldn't you offer to buy the others?"

"Yes, but they refused. I even offered them more money for them."

"Tell them that the paintings are only bad magic for those who believe in it…and try offering them even more money. In the mean time, I'm impressed. We have enough paintings here for an exhibition."

A small, hastily planned exhibition of Jimmy Snakespirit's work had been presented a few months later and was a great success. William Price returned to the South Woods and purchased a large number of paintings and presented a second exhibition. Despite raising the prices, all of the pieces sold. Now, he wondered why he ever bothered to send a Jimmy Snakespirit painting to a small time dealer in Los Angeles. The artist's career was taking off and there was no reason to send any more work his way. The exhibitions had gotten excellent reviews and he'd managed to raise the prices 200% in less than a year's time. His discovery had turned out very well and he was hoping to debut the artist's strongest body of work in the coming months.

Sleeping Passengers

Marcia and Lenny Mitchell were both asleep, and it began to rain lightly. As Brad drove, he glanced at Marcia and thought it odd that she would be the one. She was beautiful and intelligent, and he never thought he would end up with some one like her. In fact he was beginning to doubt that he would ever have anyone. Brad imagined that he might grow old and wander through town, hearing people whisper "there goes the lonely fool" behind his back. Now, he thought it possible that he might go to his twenty year high school reunion. With a girl like her, he would be proud.

Driving through rural America, one sees places which have been abandoned. In Europe such places go back centuries, but in America it's often a matter of decades. Towns that grew for a time, then fell upon tough economic times and dried up. Factories that thrived for a time, then fell victim to the economy or progress. Gas stations that have been deserted due to a poor choice of location or an ended relationship. Shops or houses where people just up and left, allowing the place to vacantly fall apart over the years. It always caused Brad to wonder about the people; who they were and why they left. And it made him think of home. The North Woods were filled with such places and he knew the ghosts who belonged to them.

Spending so much time out in the woods and in the company of Natives caused Brad to feel he'd grown up in a different century. Years later, befriending old Mr. Ellison at the Historical Society reinforced this. Brad's Grandmother, who dragged him to services at a country church, was also largely responsible. Those people, with their place and means of worship, seemed terribly out of place with modern pop culture. Labeling so much of it evil, they avoided most of modern life and chose to live in another time.

As most of the townspeople shared this country church, they managed to keep the entire town a century or two back. It was not exactly that they lived in the past, but they maintained Victorian lives, sustaining what they believed to be the good old days.

The town Brad spent his life in was very small, consisting of a gas station, a small market and a bar. The lakes and woods had always made it a popular resort area and there were a few motels. There was also the Historical Society. Strangely enough this little town had once been a major center of life for people in the North Woods. Years later, there remained only old photos, letters and the diaries of it's inhabitants; and an old cemetery where the population was much larger than the living population. The Historical Society, housed in an old building where it had passed through decades, had long existed by the devotion of an old man named Mr. Ellison.

Brad would usually stop by the Historical Society to visit Mr. Ellison on his way to work. Often, he would leave early, so that they could play a game of chess. Even if he was running behind, he would stop by however, in case the old man needed anything in town. The local market was limited as to what they could supply. Mr. Ellison liked dark chocolate and a particular wine. It was a burgundy, sold by the jug, but only carried by the supermarket in Bay Springs. Mr. Ellison claimed that the chocolate and wine were the secret to his long life. Brad was sure that it actually had a lot to do with his long walks and positive attitude. Still, just to be on the safe side, Brad ate his share of chocolate.

He preferred beer to wine however, even though he'd heard about a study that proved that it shrunk the brain. Brad didn't see that as a problem, as any unhappiness in his life came from too much thinking and the consideration of the rather odd aspects of his life.

The Gift

The summer after Brad received the gift, he was living an ordinary life. There had been a couple of experiences where he'd had visions of the dead, but he had written them off as bad day dreams. He figured that it was odd to have such realistic day dreams, but was trying to convince myself that this was the case. It was preferable to considering that he might be mentally ill, like his Aunt and a few extended members of the family.

There had been two experiences. The first time was at the library. Brad was about to check out an old book and found the signature of it's original owner inside the cover. He ran his finger across it and suddenly there was the man, introducing himself. Brad closed the book and put it back, then made his exit from the library. He didn't return for a couple of years.

The second time, Brad walked into the den to find his mother going through some old papers.

"Oh my...look at this." She called out to him. "It's a letter written by your Great Grandmother to her sister."

She looked the letter over, then handed it to Brad. Taking it in his hands, he suddenly saw his Great Grandmother standing there smiling at him.

"How are you?" She asked.

"Fine." He said and handed the letter back to his mother.

Once he became accustomed to it, the way Brad's gift worked was this: he would take any sample of a deceased persons handwriting and close his eyes. Within a moment he would find himself in the company of that person. He always found that they would be easy to get along with, if at times a bit confused and curious why he was there and what he wanted. Brad conversed with them, though nothing was evident to anyone who witnessed the experience. To them, he seemed to be just sitting there with his eyes closed.

Brad always tried to keep the gift a secret, and almost every time he used it he was alone with Mr. Ellison at the Historical Society. Mr. Ellison had him go back and ask people about their lives, to assist him in genealogies and a history of the county. Often, he wanted Brad to check in with old friends of his. Mr. Ellison loved to tell stories of the old days and Brad suspected that he wanted him to know the people as well as he did. They shared friends and, to a certain degree, Brad was able to live in the past with Mr. Ellison.

On several occasions, Brad communicated with members of his own family. He had the opportunity to meet his great-grand-parents and his great-great-grandparents. People seemed unwilling or unable to talk about life on the other side. Rather they spoke of the things that they had shared; weather, family and life in the North Woods.

Although he found some comfort in his gift and the knowledge that the dead lived, Brad always hoped that it would one day be gone. Once he became accustom to the experience, it was never frightening, as one would suspect. Yet, conversing with the dead wasn't ordinary and it made him feel uncomfortable.

Mr. Ellison had found an old land deed, with the signature of Brad's great grandfather. Brad had never met him, but his father had told him stories about him as he grew up. The man was a true pioneer and had been the member of the family who originally settled in the North Woods. Brad was never certain that he wanted to communicate with his deceased relatives, as he was never sure what to say, or what they wanted to hear. After all, he wasn't ever sure how to deal with his living relatives. Mr. Ellison always had an excuse, a reason why he wanted Brad to do it. In this case it was to help with some genealogies he was working on; information about the names of the neighbors and the names of their children if he remembered any of them.

"Well, hello." Great Grandpa Virgil said, after Brad had introduced myself. "How are you?"

"I'm just fine." Brad replied.

"And how's the farm?..." He asked, making reference to a place Brad was unfamiliar with. Brad's father had bought the land they lived on when he was a child and had never mentioned a family farm.

"Fine." Brad lied, going back over the family stories in his mind and trying to remember when and where there had been a farm.

"I worked hard to build that place up..." He went on. "But it was worth it knowing that I was creating a home for my children and their children..."

Brad didn't want to discuss the farm with him. He figured that it had probably been one of his own children, who had sold the place and moved away. Perhaps it had been hard times or bad luck or they had just decided to move off to the city. Brad's father had never talked about it. Perhaps there were hard feelings. It was possible that it had all just been forgotten.

Although the farm had probably been in the immediate vicinity, Brad didn't want to learn where it was. Another family had probably come to call the place home or it had been abandoned. He considered that a time might come when his family house or his place in the tree would be the home of strangers. It was hard to imagine a world so different. Brad considered that perhaps this might be the reason why those on the other side seemed unaware of what was happening in the world.

Some people believe that their ancestors watch over them like guardian angels, always ready to advise and assist them. It had been Brad's experience that people didn't cease to be people and that those who came before were unaware and unable to comprehend change. Mr. Ellison was raised a Baptist, but had long ago chosen long walks in the woods over church attendance. Once he became aware of Brad's gift, he wanted very much to understand exactly where the dead were. Issues of Heaven and Hell were not proven or disproved, as the deceased always avoided answering questions regarding life on the other side. It seemed to Brad that these souls were in some sort of waiting area and he found they were usually in pretty good spirits.

Brad told his Great Grandpa Virgil that he had come for a purpose, to ask him the questions Mr. Ellison had provided. They talked at length about the people, but the subject often returned to his life on the farm. Brad managed to tell him only the most positive aspects of their lives, and to avoid telling him anything that would reveal the absence of the family farm. It was his life's work, after all, and most cherished memory of the world he had left behind.

Understanding the Opposite Sex

Brad Mitchell passed through adolescence with his odd gift and a generally romantic view of life. Sex and religion were certainly mysteries, yet he suspected that this was meant to be. He established a pattern of spending most of his free time in his tree house, reading and writing. He avoided doing homework, as he thought himself too intelligent to waste his time doing it. He preferred to pass his time alone and occasionally enjoyed a cigarette and a beer. Brad's older brother had been kind enough to point out to him that his father rarely noticed when either had been pilfered and he came to keep a small stockpile of each.

One summer day, while Brad was sitting on the tree house porch, listening to the radio and writing in his notebook, he noticed his father walking up the porch toward him. He quickly hid the beer he had been sipping and looking relaxed and happy to see him, smiled and waved. Lenny Mitchell had been drinking a bit himself, this being evidenced by his not calculating a curve in the trail and tripping over an exposed root. Brad heard his father's head hit a tree, but he regained his balance with some ease and grace and walked up the steps and sat down beside his son. Lenny Mitchell had brought a six pack of beer with him and pulled off two cans. He popped both open and handed one to Brad.

"Here you go." He said. "I think that you're old enough to have a beer."

"Thanks." Brad said taking it.

"Furthermore…" Lenny Mitchell started. "I think it's time we had a talk."

Brad was concerned. A beer and a talk. It sounded very serious. It wasn't really that Brad was concerned that he had done something wrong, but rather that he would have to figure out what his father had found out about.

"What do you want to talk about?" Brad asked.

"Well, your mom thinks it's time you and I had a little talk about the birds and the bees. Now, I'm sure that you already know all about sex. Heck, you could probably teach me a thing or two. What I feel you should be aware of are the, um, psychological factors…"

"How do you mean?"

"It's like this…Women sometimes behave like alien creatures, but it's important that you always remember that they are human beings…"

Lenny Mitchell looked at Brad, to make certain that he was following, then continued.

"Now, your mother…she's different. That's why I married her. But a lot of women can be very difficult. It's a biological thing that leads to psychological situations. An extreme case would be someone like Lizzie Borden. Now then, what a man needs to do is pay attention…to avoid that type of thing…"

"But Lizzie Borden was crazy wasn't she?"

"Not necessarily…women can do worse and feel fully justified. Later, they might say that they're sorry and that they were just so pissed off…but in a situation like that, it's too late. That's why you have to always pay attention to a woman's moods. So that you can be careful what you say and when you say it."

Brad didn't really believe his father, but he was young and didn't know for sure. He'd never had any solid biological facts explained to him and had to figure it out from magazines and the stories his friends told. Brad considered that much of what his friends believed was even more confused than what his father told him. If everything that he had been told about women was true, he would have thought them to be monster Goddesses. Local men often said things such as, "she's messing with my mind something awful" or "she really knows how to get me to do what she wants." Although the men liked to act very tough and independent, it was apparent that they were under the control of women.

Brad found early on that he liked women very much, although he was a little afraid of them. Perhaps he suspected that the local women might be as his father described and this had something to do with why he found himself waiting for the perfect girl to appear in town.

Last Chance

Thomas Reed awoke one Saturday morning, expecting to put in a half a day at the office. Having closed down the bars with a few of his friends from the office, he was terribly hung over. Yet, he knew what a good impression working on the weekend made on his boss, Mr. Jacobs. Marcia had been very upset with him. She had apparently prepared a special dinner, expecting him to come home. He'd asked his secretary to call and tell her that he would be late, of course, but he'd been later than he'd estimated. When he finally got home they had argued. As far as he was concerned, it was hardly his fault.

He looked at the clock on the nightstand to find that it was ten a.m. He had set the alarm, planning on being at the office by nine, but it hadn't gone off. He wondered why Marcia hadn't awakened him. She knew what time he liked to go in on Saturdays. He managed to sit up and rested his face in his hands.

"Marcia!" He called out. A moment passed, then a minute and she didn't answer. He opened his eyes and looked around the room. The drapes were pulled and it was dark. He got up and walked over to let in the sun, turning away like a vampire as he opened the drapes.

"Marcia!" He called out again. He started across the room, then stopped, noticing an envelope on her pillow. He picked it up and made his way to the kitchen. He knew what the letter said. She had left him again. He was hoping that she'd been kind enough to brew a pot of coffee before doing so, but making his way to the coffee maker he knew this was not the case.

She had been so upset the night before and he figured that he should stop to read the letter, to get a feel for what exactly her problem was. If Marcia wasn't too mad, she would be back by the time he got home from the office. If she was really angry with him, he would find her at his mother's house. It was where she had a tendency to go. She had no family in the city and her own mother had died when she was a child. Usually, he would have to buy her roses and call to apologize and explain. His mother wouldn't defend him, but she would do her best to convince Marcia to go back to him. Thomas sat the unopened envelope on the table and went to take a shower. There was still time to put in an appearance at the office and work a few hours.

On Sunday, Thomas again woke up alone and looked at the clock. He realized that the game was on and got up and went to turn on the television. He made coffee, which he realized tasted horrible. He heated up the dinner which Marcia had left in the refrigerator Friday night. It was delicious. After he finished eating, he went to the telephone and made a call.

"Hello mom?"

"Hello Thomas. How are you?"

"Um, fine. Thanks."

"And how's Marcia?"

"Isn't she there?"

"What do you mean? I thought you two were together…she said that you were getting out of town for the weekend."

"She said what?…"

"She stopped by Friday night and borrowed my suitcase…"

Marcia Roberts was in the kitchen of her family home, her first time back in the North Woods in nearly a decade. The phone rang, and she went to answer it, with no idea that it might be Thomas. He was happy to catch her. Sitting at his desk with a view of the New York Skyline, he smiled as he spoke, as though it would make him more charming.

"Hello, Marcia?…It's Thomas."

"Thomas…hello. What a surprise. How did you get my number here?"

"You left it with Mr. Jacobs." He wanted me to call, and of course, I wanted to talk to you…" Thomas spun his chair around as he spoke, not at all as concerned as he hoped to make her think. "What I…and what we all want to know…Is when are you coming back?"

"I don't know." Marcia sat down with her tea. This was difficult for her.

"Well, this leave of absence thing is very confusing. You never even mentioned to me that you were taking a leave of absence from work. It's hard to tell if you're gone for good or just on vacation…"

"I'm confused myself." Marcia had hoped that she wouldn't hear from him so soon, as she hadn't had time to consider what she would say.

"There's so much going on here in the city." Thomas went on. "I can't imagine that there is much going on out there in the boondocks…"

"Actually it's kind of nice here." Marcia considered that she might tell him that she was staying, although she wasn't really sure of it. "Whether I could ever live back here, I don't know…But then, I don't know that I want to spend the rest of my life there either."

"Listen." Thomas stopped spinning his chair around. Not smiling, and looking rather sincere, he spoke softly. "Can we talk about us? I know we fought, but you know me honey…I think that you're asking me to understand things that you don't understand yourself…"

"And that's why I needed some time to be alone." Her guard was up, as he was talking like Thomas now.

"I can't imagine someone leaving New York City to find the meaning of life. You've got it all here…It doesn't make sense."

"Listen Thomas…I've got to go."

Marcia hung up the phone. Angry and sad, she went back over to her tea.

The Historical Society

Brad pulled up in the empty parking lot and went inside. Mr. Ellison greeted him with a smile as always and gestured toward the chess table by the window.

"I don't suppose you have time for a game?" He was aware that Brad was running late and Brad could see that he was disappointed.

"No...I have to work. I just wanted to check in and see if you needed anything from town."

"No, I'm fine." Mr. Ellison smiled and nodded and sat down at his desk. "Maybe tomorrow we'll play a game."

"Sure." Brad said.

Walking out to his car, Brad knew that he would make time to visit with Mr. Ellison the following afternoon and play a game of chess. He had learned a great deal from the old man about life and living. He'd lived longer than anyone else Brad knew and had seen a great deal. Yet, as wise as Brad found him, he was aware that the world had remained a mystery to him. Brad pulled out of the dusty driveway and started down the highway.

Marcia Roberts drove down the road to town. She pulled up in front of the Historical Society and found Mr. Ellison inside, at his desk. He hadn't heard her enter and sat looking at an old album.

"Hi, are you open?..."

Mr. Ellison looked up at her, surprised, then back at one of the photos for a moment. His finger rested on the face of the girl in a sepia tone photo, who smiled out at him.

"Oh, yes, hello." He got up and started across the room. "What can I do for you young lady?"

"My name is Marcia Roberts. My family has a place out on old Simmons Road…it's been in the family for generations."

"The Roberts family…yes." Mr. Ellison knew everything about the area, although it took time for all of the memories to fully surface. He realized that Christine was a member of the family and thought it an odd coincidence.

"By chance, did you know my grandparents, Bill and Thelma?"

"Knew of them, but I didn't know them personally. I knew Thelma's sister Christine…Matter of fact, I just came upon a picture of her here in this photo album."

Marcia walked over and looked at the photo, as he held the book out for her. Now that he was standing close to her, he could see her very well. She was quite attractive. He wished that his sense of smell was better, that he could smell her perfume. He wished that he was younger, so that when he smiled, she would be flattered.

"She would have been my great Aunt." Marcia studied the photo for a moment, not taking in the similarities that Mr. Ellison was so aware of. "Funny…I've never heard of her."

"Well, she ran off to the city, right after graduation." He took another look at the photo, then shut the book and set it on the desk.

"My grandfather had a brother, named Claude…do you know anything about him?"

"Can't say as I do…"

"He was a gangster, I hear." She offered.

"Well, then he must have run off to the city too. Can't say as I know about any gangsters who lived around these parts."

"Is there a way to research any of this?"

"Sure. I'll look into it for you..." Mr. Ellison made his way over to the desk, and found his glasses, pen and paper. "Let me write these names down here..."

"Thanks." Marcia smiled. "I really appreciate it."

A New York Exhibition

The Werner/Price Gallery was designed like a sanctuary and the Jimmy Snakespirit exhibition was hung to reflect this. Small paintings lined the walls, like the stations of the cross, with a group of large paintings hung against the far wall.

Leah Sauer was the daughter of a well known art critic and the Village Voice had sent her to review the exhibition. She had woke up with the man she had been trying to seduce for a year. With his girlfriend out of town, he had called her and suggested they go out for a drink. After drinks they had gone to his place and she had found him to be extremely passionate.

"It's been a long time." He explained.

"But she's only been gone a few days." Leah said.

"Yes…" Thomas got up to take a shower. "…I know."

Once he was in the shower, Leah got out of bed and went to join him. It seemed the beginning of a great relationship.

Now, looking at paintings together, he seemed distant.

"What are you thinking about?" She asked him, as he stood looking at the centerpiece of the show, a large, complex composition.

Thomas was thinking about Marcia, but he decided not to say so. He didn't want to think about her, so he turned and kissed Leah.

"Nothing." He said.

They went back to looking at the paintings. William Price came out of his office and stood watching them. The girl looked familiar. He didn't recognize them as collectors however and assumed they were just looking.

"Oh my god…" Thomas had stopped in front of a small painting and was examining it closely.

"What?" Leah walked over to him.

"The girl in this painting…she looks just like Marcia."

"Yeah, a little bit I guess…" Leah said, taking a quick look, and starting to walk away.

"No, exactly…I could swear that it is her."

William Price decided to come over and introduce himself. The young man seemed quite interested in the painting and was perhaps interested in purchasing it.

"Hello…Let me know if I can answer any questions." He said.

"Oh, Mr. Price…hello, I'm Leah Sauer." Leah stepped forward to introduce herself.

"Leah, yes, my gosh I didn't recognize you." Mr. Price was surprised to find that she was a grown woman. "I haven't seen you for years…how's your father?"

"Oh, he's fine…I'm following in his footsteps. I'm working freelance…doing some art reviews for the Village Voice."

"Will you be reviewing this show?"

She nodded.

"Ah, excellent." He said. "I'd be happy to supply you with information about Jimmy Snakespirit. He's a wonderful artist and has a fascinating story."

Thomas continued to examine the painting.

"This is my friend Thomas." She said.

Thomas turned to look at William Price.

"What can you tell me about this painting?" He asked.

"Ah, well, first of all are you familiar with the artist's work?"

"No." Leah said. "He's new on the scene, isn't he?…"

Thomas only wanted to hear about this one painting, but realized that he would have to listen to the entire history. He went back to examining it.

"Jimmy Snakespirit is by definition a southern primitive, although there is obviously a relationship to a variety of schools including abstract expressionism and surrealism evident. He calls these paintings "good luck" paintings, and believes that each one tells the story of the person who is destined to possess it. The only exception in this exhibition is that particular painting…"

"Yeah?…" Thomas turned to look at him. "So, what's the story with this one?"

"Well, Jimmy apparently can't read his own paintings and his grandmother, a sort of medicine woman, interprets them for him. When she saw this one, she told him that it was actually his future. That the couple in the painting would soon be coming to visit him and it would forever change his life. Hence the title…Soon they will come".

"Wow." Leah said.

"How much is this one?" Thomas asked.

"It's one of the smallest ones in the show, and therefore one of the most affordable." William Price explained. "It's priced at twenty five hundred."

As was the case with each of the paintings he'd sold by the artist, he calculated in his head the profit margin. He'd paid fifty dollars for this particular one.

"Can I put a deposit on my credit card?" Thomas asked.

"Ah, certainly." Came the answer.

Bay Springs

It was an ordinary day. After stopping by to visit Mr. Ellison, Brad drove on into Bay Springs to work. Walking past the lingerie store, Mary came out and stopped him. He'd known Mary since grade school and saw her almost everyday in town.

"Can you come in?" She asked.

"Aunt Jane again?" Brad asked, not needing to. He found her standing in the aisle wearing a black slip and feather boa.

Brad's mother's sister, his Aunt Jane, lived with the family. She was the reason his mother said she was unable to get a job and had to spend most of her time at home.

"Aunt Jane is unbalanced." Mother explained to Brad. "I'm not sure if it's a chemical thing or if it's the years she spent with our Uncle Sam…You've just got to be patient with her."

Brad's maternal grandfather died when his mother was a still a child. She and her sister Jane were raised by Corporal Samuel Ellis, his elderly brother. A wounded war hero, and fiercely patriotic, it was Samuel who had convinced his little brother to join the army and go off to war. He was damn proud of his brother for having died on the battlefield and he worked to enlist others long after his official retirement. His hair was white and when he grew a goatee, everyone was convinced that he looked the very image of Uncle Sam. That's what people came to call him and he dressed and acted the part, touring the Midwest to promote the armed services.

It was not expected of Sarah and Jane to marry a soldier, but they were encouraged to date, dine and dance with them until the time they did marry. It seemed to Uncle Sam that this was the way a woman could best serve her country—to bring a little sunshine into the lives of men who would go off and fight for their country. He believed that if every beautiful woman made it known that she preferred the company of a soldier and looked to marry one, they would be doing their country a great service and a mighty military would be established.

Lenny Mitchell was not at all what Uncle Sam had in mind for Sarah. She of course realized this and did everything she could to put off their meeting. She asked Lenny if perhaps he had some desire to join the military; that was, if his musical career didn't pan out. This was the last thing he wanted to do with his life. After all, he was a lover, not a fighter.

Brad's mother ended up betraying her Uncle Sam and marrying Lenny Mitchell and this was her salvation. Aunt Jane was not so fortunate. By the time Uncle Sam passed away, she was an old maid. For the next twenty years she was the town tramp, making up for lost time. Years later, she was Brad's crazy aunt.

Aunt Jane would often go into town. She would spend all of her Social Security money and, even when it was gone, she shopped and tried on clothing at the stores almost daily, with a preference for lingerie. It was often Brad's responsibility to bring her home and all of the sales girls in town knew him by name.

"Why don't you call Charlie at the plant..." Brad suggested, as he had to open up the pizza parlor and didn't have the time. "He'll be getting off soon, and he can take her home."

"I'll call Charlie." One of the sales girls volunteered, going to the phone. Brad remembered seeing her at the bar with Charlie one night. A guy like Charlie in a town like theirs, always had a girlfriend. Mary and Brad walked outside.

"So, how are things going between Charlie and Tina?"

"They still haven't spoken to each other." He shrugged. "Aside from that, it's better then it used to be. They don't have those terrible arguments any more."

"I hear that you and Tina might be an item...that you've been seen at the movies and places together."

"Oh no, we're just friends...She's like family." Joey Lewis drove by then, in his pink hearse. He honked, and they waved to him. Joey worked hard at being a town character and everyone seemed to like him. "Listen, I've got to get to work. I'll see you."

"Bye." Mary said, pouting a little. Brad always suspected that she was flirting a bit with him, but he was never certain. Being somewhat shy and not understanding women at all, he always went on his way.

Brad unlocked the front door of the pizzeria, and went in. He turned on the oven, the lights, and the music. Tim walked in just after him.

"Ready for your first day on the job?" Brad asked.

"I think so."

"Good. Let's take a break."

Knowing that the ovens needed time to warm up and everything was on schedule, Brad decided to take the time for a talk and to explain his philosophy of work. He'd had the same talk with many employees over the years and called it his "Live in the Moment in a Small Town" lecture. He continued to refine it on every new employee, although no one ever seemed sure of what he was getting at, nor did they ever stay too long. Brad had tried putting it in writing, but reading it he realized that it didn't seem to make any sense. He supposed that it should remain an oral tradition. Brad was never sure why people had an inability to look at making pizza for the residents of Bay Springs as a career, as it seemed as good a job as any to him.

Brad realized that most people wanted more, although he'd never understood why. He considered Randy's ambitions and a memory came to him. They were sixteen years of age, sitting on the porch of the tree house one Indian Summer evening. Randy had his guitar on his lap and was going through one of Brad's recent notebooks, looking for poems that he could turn into songs.

"I've got an idea." Randy had said.

"What's that?"

"Let's write a musical…"

"Sounds like a line from one of those old MGM movies that mom and Aunt Jane like so much…"

"No, I mean like a rock opera." He went on. "All the songs we've written together…we could put them together so that they tell a story. Hell, they tell a story anyway…the story of your life."

"Oh great. A musical based on my life…People would certainly stand in line for that one."

"You would be famous…"

"Well, that's the difference between us…you want to go off to the city and make it big, so that everyone will know who you are. Me, I just want to stay here in the North Woods and write and be left alone."

"Well, if you're a famous author, people will know who you are…"

"Yeah, well I'm not sure that I want to be that successful…maybe they could leave my photo off the book jacket or I could write under a pseudonym…"

"What purpose would that serve?" Randy asked. "Anyway, I like the idea of a musical and I don't care what you think. One day I'll take a bunch of your lyrics and put them together and write music and you'll say—wow, what a great idea that was of Randy's…"

"Yeah, alright. Just include me out."

Meeting Marcia

Brad was in a rather odd state of mind when he met Marcia Roberts. It seemed that his world was falling apart, although he later learned that it was actually falling together. Marcia was in a state of analytical unknowing herself, which made it the best time for them to meet up. It was Brad's cousin Charlie who brought her into his life. Charlie lived with the family, offering very little help. He was probably as intelligent as anyone in the North Woods, yet like so many he preferred to coast through life as much as possible.

"I work hard all day..." He would always say. "...and all that I ask is that I be allowed to come home and have a few beers and relax."

Charlie married Tina straight out of high school and had been regretting it ever since. She had been pregnant and, although they had a wonderful child, they weren't meant to be together at all. Tina was too smart for Charlie and she was definitely too opinionated.

Charlie and Tina had been separated for over a year, but she had no where to go. Charlie wouldn't divorce her or pay for any of their expenses, unless she apologized to him for being so disagreeable. Tina refused to speak to him. She had a part time job and paid her way, sharing a room with the baby.

Brad liked Tina. Sometimes they would go into town to see a movie together. She'd been the closest thing he'd had to a date in years and they enjoyed one another's company. She seemed like a sister to him and he saw no possibility of romance or sex between them. He was also very fond of the baby and prayed every night that she wouldn't grow up to be odd. Of course, he prayed the same for his own future, believing that it might one day contain a greater amount of normalcy.

Charlie and Brad had very little in common, and had disagreements regarding financial matters. Brad was sure that it was this way with many extended families. He would occasionally sit on the porch, have a beer with Charlie and discuss life in their little town. Charlie often inquired whether or not Brad found Tina attractive. Brad always insisted that he didn't and that he respected the fact that she was still Charlie's wife.

It was Brad's day off, and he and Charlie were sitting on the back porch drinking beer and having what seemed to be another of their pointless conversations.

"You could have her if you want her." Charlie said, changing the subject suddenly. Brad realized that he was talking about his wife Tina. He found the statement surprising and confusing and was sure that it showed on his face. "What I mean is, well…I know that she likes you."

"And I like her." Brad explained. "But not in that way."

"She's actually pretty good in the sack.

"That's none of my business."

"Could be if you wanted."

"But I don't."

Charlie nodded, lit a cigarette and said nothing for a few minutes.

"It's sort of insulting." He said finally. "To me and to her."

"I don't mean it to be…that is, I'm trying to be respectful of you both."

"Well, it kind of suggests that you don't think that she's an attractive woman or that maybe I have bad taste."

"But she is attractive." Brad was trying to explain it all in a manner that wouldn't lead to one of Charlie's violent episodes and to find a way out of the conversation. "When I marry, I hope that it's to someone like her."

"But not her."

"No not her."

"You think I don't know a good woman when I see one?…Or that I have an inability to get one?" He was getting worked up, and turning red a little bit. "Come on…"

Charlie got up and started down the driveway.

"Where?"

"You'll see." Brad finished his beer and followed him. Charlie finished his beer and they threw their cans into the trash can in the driveway. It was always there for that purpose, because the family had always been opposed to drinking and driving. They got in his truck and took off down the road.

"Do you know the Robert's family?" Charlie asked, as he drove ever faster, rarely looking at the road ahead.

"Yeah, they live about a mile from here…they have a little place set back in the woods."

"Do you know their girl, Cyndi?"

"The retarded one?"

Charlie looked confused for a moment, then very serious.

"She's retarded?…" He asked, shrugging his shoulders. "She seems normal."

"Physically yes." Brad explained. "In fact, she's quite an attractive girl. But she's mentally…sort of simple, or something."

"Oh, so you find her physically attractive?…"

"Sure, she's very pretty."

Charlie smiled and drove a little faster, sitting a little higher in his seat.

"She's my new girlfriend." He said, watching Brad's face as he said it, so he could see how impressed he was. "And I need your help…"

"What can I do for you?" He was very happy and being very nice now. Despite the fact that they didn't really like each other, Brad felt that they were family and that he should want to help his cousin.

"You know her sister?"

"I don't know…what's her name?"

"I'm not sure."

Brad tried, but couldn't think of who she was.

"Her sister doesn't like me." Charlie explained. "And I feel that she doesn't trust me."

"In what sense?"

"She won't leave me alone with Cyndi…It's like she's afraid that I'll take advantage of her."

"Well, Charlie…I must admit that seems a possibility doesn't it? I mean, I know that you don't have a lot of control in that department."

"Well, yeah…" Charlie waved his hands in the air. The car swerved a bit, but he quickly brought it back under control. "But she's a grown woman…she can think for herself…"

"But, she is mentally…you know…retarded."

"Well, I think you might be wrong about that. I mean, she's a little bit short of brains…but that's the way I like my women."

"I think that Tina is very intelligent." Brad offered.

"Yeah, well I think that's the problem with Tina." Charlie was getting angry again. Brad didn't say anything and Charlie didn't say anything else. A few minutes later they were pulling down the driveway that led to a cabin in the woods.

Cyndi was sitting on a bench in front, in a bikini top, blue denim cutoffs and pigtails. She looked like a woman and she looked like a little girl and Brad could tell that Charlie liked that. Charlie parked the truck and walked over to her. By the time Brad got out of the car, Cyndi's sister was out of the cabin and standing on the steps watching them. She didn't seem to notice Brad, as he walked over to where Charlie and Cyndi were standing.

"See what I mean?" Charlie asked, motioning toward the sister.

Brad nodded. He hadn't got a good look at her yet, but could sense that she was a force to be reckoned with.

"The favor that I need you to do, is to keep her sister busy…Cyndi and I want to go for a walk in the cornfields. Isn't that right honey?" He smiled at her and she giggled and couldn't bring herself to look at Brad.

Brad nodded. It meant that he understood, but not necessarily that he would go along with it. Although it was quite possible that Charlie and Cyndi were soul mates, he wasn't convinced that it was the right thing for him to promote.

"Don't you think that she's beautiful?" Charlie asked. She looked at Brad and she smiled. Cyndi was actually quite attractive, yet she seemed like a child, despite her being well endowed.

Brad nodded. It meant that he wanted to be polite, but not that he went along with Charlie taking her off into the corn-fields and having his way with her. Yet, Brad watched as they walked off together, then walked over to where her sister Marcia was standing.

"Hi, I'm Brad. I'm Charlie's cousin."

"What's going on?" Marcia looked him over once quickly, then her eyes returned to the two of them, making their way past the family lot. Brad didn't know what to say, so said nothing until she spoke again. "I'm responsible for her."

"I'm not responsible for him." He said quickly, as a disclaimer, not considering that it suggested that Charlie was as untrustworthy as he knew him to be.

"Let's go for a walk." She said, as they set out after them.

"Sure." Brad nodded and walked with her, taking the opportunity to take in her appearance. She was dressed very casually. Her hair flowed from a baseball cap on to her shoulders and it looked as though she was braless under her tee shirt, which was tucked into a worn out pair of jeans. There was no doubt that she was a beautiful woman and as well built as her sister, although dressed to downplay it.

"I'm Marcia." She introduced herself as they walked, being quite courteous, despite her concern. "Nice to meet you."

"Nice to meet you…You didn't grow up here did you?"

"No, they sent me away to school."

Brad suppose that he must have looked at her in a way that suggested that it was bad to be sent away; that she must have been a juvenile delinquent.

"When I was a little girl, I scored extremely high on IQ tests…" She explained. "There was an experimental school in Detroit, funded by the state, and they sent me there."

"Wow…so you're a genius?…"

"Not at all. As it turned out, as I got older, my IQ got lower and by the time I graduated from college I was just average." She continued to watch Charlie and Cyndi, who had disappeared into the cornfields. "Let's walk a little faster."

"So what do you do now?"

"I've come here to stay with my dad and sister. I'll just be here for a few months, to sort of relax and decide what to do…and to hunt for buried treasure…"

She glanced at Brad to see if he was going to make a remark about the buried treasure. He wasn't sure what she was talking about, although he would soon find himself assisting her with it. He nodded to let her know that he was listening and interested in what she had to say.

"After college I went to work as an editor in a New York publishing house." She continued. "There's talk that I'm due to be promoted up the ladder, which would pay a lot but give me a hellish work schedule...and I need to decide if that's what I want to do..."

"Oh, an average job for an average person..."

"Well, I didn't say I wasn't bright...I just didn't want for you to think I was some sort of genius or freak because I went to a special school."

Marcia stopped walking, having reached the edge of the cornfield. "I don't know how we'll find them in there."

"Don't worry about it." Brad said. "She'll be okay...Charlie is harmless."

"Yes." She said in a short, sharp, rather unhappy manner. "But Charlie is also married and I don't want for him to get her pregnant."

"Actually, Charlie is separated." Brad said in defense of his cousin.

"They still live together." She shot back. She wasn't looking at Brad now as though she thought very much of him. Her look suggested that she was thinking he was helping Charlie or that it was his intention for all of them to go off into the cornfield to have a family orgy.

"How do you know so much about us?"

"Everybody in town knows about your family." She said, returning her attention to the cornfield.

"I hope that they say nice things."

"Let's go." She said, leading him into the cornfield.

"You know…it's interesting that you edit books." Brad said as they walked, bent over, between the stalks. "Because I'm an aspiring writer."

"Do you write?" She asked.

"Yes." He said.

"Then you are a writer…You might be aspiring to be published, or aspiring to be good, but if you write you are a writer."

"Yes, that's true." Brad said, not certain if she was complimenting him or talking to him as though he were an idiot.

They surprised a couple of rabbits, almost stepping on them as they did what they do. They ran off, scared and in search of a better place.

"It's good that you write. You have a very literary family…" Marcia said, after giving him a few moments to think.

"Thank you." Brad said, as they came upon Charlie and Cyndi, laying half clothed in the dirt.

"Cyndi!…" Marcia screamed. "What did I tell you?…"

"About what?" Cyndi asked, climbing to her feet.

"I told you that he was married!…"

"Yeah, but he doesn't have a wife…" Cyndi explained, dressing herself slowly. It was easy for Brad to see why Charlie was having problems with self control. Brad gestured for him to pull up his pants and he did so, quite surprised that he had stood up and left them down.

"Of course he has a wife." Marcia put her arm around her sister and started leading her away.

"He doesn't…it's sort of confusing the way he explains it…but…"

"Well, damn it, thanks for all your help cousin!…" Charlie yelled at Brad, causing Marcia to turn around and give him a terribly nasty look.

Brad shrugged and smiled at her, but didn't think that it helped.

"Let's go." Brad said, and they started out of the cornfield, after the women.

"He says that if he didn't love me, he wouldn't be able to make love to me." They heard Cyndi say. Brad looked at Charlie, raising an eyebrow. Charlie looked back and shrugged as if to say that he sincerely believed it.

"Sometimes men can make us think that dear..." Marcia was saying. "But if they actually come out and say it, you can't believe them."

Brad and Charlie walked out of the cornfield. As the women heading toward the cabin, they went toward the truck. Brad didn't know if Charlie loved her. He didn't know if it would have been right or wrong if he did, although he still believed that Charlie and Tina could work things out. What Brad did know, was that he liked Marcia Roberts very much and that he seemed to her a bad guy. He felt like a fool, and considered something he had once read; that love made people stupid. That would certainly explain Charlie, he thought, as well as his inability to say or do the right thing in the company of Marcia Roberts.

Losing a Friend

Brad stopped by the Historical Society on his way to work. He pulled in the drive and started up the steps. There was a creak in the step, which caused him to stop. He'd first noticed it a few months before. He had been walking up the steps, about to go in, when Joey Lewis pulled up in his pink hearse. He remembered thinking it strange and wondering what he was doing there. Walking across the drive to his car window, Brad noticed that Susan Fisher was sitting inside with him.

"Hey, what's up?" He asked them.

They were both the types to be always partying and smiling, yet they were sitting there with blank looks on their faces. After a moment, she got out of the car and Joey started to speak.

"I just talked to Randy's sister Beth." He said.

They seemed so out of place there at the Historical Society, being so serious.

"It's about Randy...Susan and I know how close you guys are, so we thought we should come over and tell you."

"What?..." Brad looked over at Susan. She was leaning against the front of the car, looking away each time he looked her direction.

"There was an accident...He's dead." Joey said it quickly, then leaned his head back and looked past Brad; up at the sky.

Brad didn't know what to think. Could it be some sort of joke? He'd known Joey and Susan for years, they had gone to school together. Yet, they weren't close friends and there didn't seem to be a reason why it would be them coming to tell him this. It would be a cruel joke, he thought, but it would be a terrible thing to accuse them of making up. He found some comfort in considering the possibility that it somehow wasn't true.

Brad walked over and sat on the steps of the Historical Society. Mr. Ellison had come outside and asked him what was going on. Brad didn't say anything. He felt as though he couldn't speak.

"His friend Randy was killed in an accident." Susan told him.

Joey had gotten out of his car, but had stopped to light a cigarette. Mr. Ellison came and sat down beside Brad. The old man groaned and Brad heard his bones creak. Susan sat down on the steps behind Brad. She stretched her legs down on either side of him, then leaned forward and held him. He wondered what she was expecting; whether she figured that he would lean back into her, or if he would break down in tears. He knew that it was normal to cry, yet didn't feel as though he would. He wasn't really feeling anything at that moment, except disbelief.

"Strange you coming here in your pink hearse to deliver this information." Brad said, as Joey approached. "I guess that life is sort of surreal."

"Yeah." He nodded. "You know, back when I bought it…it was our senior year of high school, and I didn't even think about death. I just thought it was a cool car because it shocked people and it was the best possible vehicle to party in."

Brad remembered when they were in school for a moment. There was a time when Randy and Brad used to hang out with Joey, and go cruising in the hearse. He had somehow forgotten those nights. The passage of time made Joey and Susan seem so distant. Yet, once they had all been very close. It was perhaps only for a year or so, but there was a summer that seemed to last a lifetime, that they had all shared.

Brad thanked Joey and Susan for coming, then walked inside the Historical Society. He heard Mr. Ellison tell them not to worry, that he would be all right. Brad watched them get into their car and wave as they drove away. Mr. Ellison walked up to the door, paused a moment and lowered his head, then came inside. Brad was sitting at the chess table. Mr. Ellison looked at him and realized that, even though he'd lived so long and seen so much, comforted so many others and lost his own friends and family, he still didn't know what to say.

"How about a game?" Brad asked. He didn't want to talk and it seemed that taking it all in would somehow be easier, if he was distracted. Mr. Ellison seemed to understand and sat down across from him.

Months later, pausing on the steps it all came back, and Brad had to wonder if it would always be that way. If he would always remember that day, when he heard the creak in the steps. If he would always feel so melancholy. Brad entered the Historical Society and found Mr. Ellison going through a bunch of old papers in a cabinet, the way he passed his days.

"Good morning." Brad smiled and waved as he stepped through the door. He was always concerned about surprising him, and perhaps scaring him, figuring that at his age his heart was probably weak and couldn't withhold too much shock.

"Marcia Roberts!" Mr. Ellison exclaimed.

"Excuse me?"

"Do you know a young lady by the name of Marcia Roberts?"

"As a matter of fact…" Brad answered.

"A very attractive young lady…" He interjected

"Yes, I would agree." Brad nodded.

"She came in here."

"She did?…What did she want?"

"Indirectly, she wants your help…" Mr. Ellison smiled. "You know, I'm surprised that you've never mentioned her."

"Well, I don't know her well…" Brad went over and stood near Mr. Ellison. "As a matter of fact, I just met her yesterday…When did she come in?"

Mr. Ellison paused, trying to remember.

"Seems as though it was yesterday…or the day before…" He said finally.

"How curious."

"Indeed…She asked me to do some research for her, and look what I found."

Mr. Ellison held up a book and lead Brad over to the table by the window. They both sat down. It's was a dusty old album, bound in red leather.

"What is it?"

"A sort of autograph book. When people had functions, such as weddings, anniversary parties or when they graduated, they would always ask everyone to write something in one of these." Mr. Ellison excitedly opened the book to the center and handed it to Brad to examine. "And look who's name is here."

Brad looked at the page. There was a short inscription:

Always, Christine Roberts

The summer of her last year of high school, Christine Roberts worked as a waitress in the cafe of the Hotel Magnificent. She would go in early to serve breakfast to the guests, the richest families from Detroit to Palm Beach. She would walk by Mr. Ellison's house on her way to and from work and he knew her shifts. He would try to time it so that he would be entering or exiting the house, or he would walk along the same route and pass her. He would take the opportunity to offer her a smile or say hello. They knew each other from school, but didn't know each other well. Aside from the business of arranging to greet her in passing, he couldn't bring himself to approach her or speak to her.

At the cafe, Christine Roberts often had men making passes at her. Some were charming and others were disgusting. Some men asked her to run away with them and others offered her money to go back to their rooms with them. As they took her to be poor, they assumed that they could take her in this manner. Christine Roberts was a shy and shocked small town girl and never knew what to make of these situations.

Within a few months of taking the job, there came a man with the right approach. He was from Chicago and told her that he could help her get into show business. She was very attractive, he explained, and could make a great deal of money. He failed to mention that he was involved in organized crime. Rather, he seemed to her a tender and romantic man. He wasn't more than a few years older than her, yet he was already a success in the world.

Mr. Ellison didn't know that this man had come to town and never really knew anything about him. He learned that Christine Roberts had run off with him a few days after she was gone, having noticed that she wasn't passing his house at the ordinary times. He asked a mutual friend about her. He knew very little about what had happened, aside from the fact that he had fallen in love with her and she was gone. He would have felt worse had he known what Christine Roberts was soon to learn; that this man was the devil.

"Your old flame." Brad said.

"You make it sound like we were lovers…" Mr. Ellison continued to stare at the page. "It wasn't like that at all."

"But you were in love with her…"

"Yes, but from afar…"

"And you wanted to marry her…and if she hadn't left town…"

"Ah, would have beens and could have beens are for the middle aged…When you get to be an old man, you just figure that it wasn't in the cards…"

"But you've been obsessed with knowing what became of her…"

"Well, I would like to know…could you?"

Brad thought about it a moment.

"What do you want to hear?…That she married someone else and bore him a dozen children?…Do you really want to know why she never came back to this town and married you?"

"Well, I always believed that she did care for me, in a way…Of course, I wish her all the best. I'd just like to know…"

Brad held the book in one hand, touching her signature and closing his eyes. He was still and silent for a moment, then opened his eyes and closed the book, handing it back to Mr. Ellison.

"I don't get anything." He hoped that Mr. Ellison wouldn't know that he was lying.

"Then she must be alive…"

"Seems to be the case…Probably a great grandma."

"Well…That's something…I guess that it just wasn't in the cards, eh?"

Brad shrugged and made the first move on the chess board. He looked out the window and found himself once again hating his gift.

"I guess." Brad said.

"I suppose that I should just get on with my life."

Although he seemed quite serious as he said it, Mr. Ellison started to smile after speaking, then began to laugh. Brad shook his head and looking at the old man, was unable to help but smile himself.

Derived from documents Mr. Ellison kept at the Historical Society, Brad had a notebook full of conversations with people involving the Hotel Magnificent, ranging from the people who lived in town to those who had vacationed there. Mr. Ellison's collection contained autographs of a number of celebrities who had played the main room and, due to his gift, Brad had the pleasure of meeting many of them. The place in time represented a whole other world and he could see why Mr. Ellison's heart and mind often went back there.

Brad was always writing, although he rarely finished anything and had no idea how he might come to be a success of it. He had been writing poetry since he was in grade school. He grew up listening to rock n' roll records and wrote in a similar lyrical style. Once Randy started to make them into songs, Brad took to supplying him with verses and a chorus. He faithfully recorded all of his experiences and had notebooks full of his time in the North Woods and conversations with Randy, Mr. Ellison and the members of his family. Brad knew and conversed with past generations of his family, stretching through the history of the place he called home.

Leaving Mr. Ellison, Brad drove to Bay Springs with the radio turned up. He'd gotten himself a good tape deck and recently installed additional speakers. He was listening to a tape Randy had sent him. He thought about their time together and Randy's rock in roll dream when he listened to it. Randy had been living in the city for over a decade and they'd fallen out of touch when the news came. That he could die was something Brad had never considered and he took it very hard. It might have had something to do with facing his own mortality, but it probably had more to do with realizing that those days were gone forever. It seemed odd that he could stay in the same place, but that time kept passing. Brad was singing along with the tape. The beauty of rock n' roll music was it's ability to put one in celebratory mood, while delivering lyrics that seemed to reflect any number of relative meanings.

Music had been everything to Randy and his guitar was his constant companion. He'd sit and play all night; singing songs that he'd written with Brad or the old Hank William's songs Lenny Mitchell had taught him. Randy and Brad listened to the rock n' roll music of their time, but when Randy sank into melancholy, he took to country music. It was in his blood, he would explain. His father had run off with another woman just after he was born and never came back to introduce himself. His mother was a tough woman and didn't waste any time thinking about such a man. She worked two jobs and, with no intention of winning any awards, tried to be a good mother. She loved Patsy Cline and sang her songs to Randy as lullabies. He grew up listening to, and took to playing, what he referred to as "white man's blues"; twangy old country songs.

When Randy died he was living with a girl named Lorna. She came back for his funeral, delivering all of his possessions to his parents, except for his notebooks and some tapes, which she hadn't been able to part with. She would sit in the home they once shared and listen to his songs and read his writing. She drank too much wine and called out to him in the night, begging him to haunt her. With time and his refusal to grant her request, her heart began to heal. She spent less time with his tapes and notebooks and found that he wasn't always on her mind. There were still times when she missed him terribly, but the occasions when she would cry in her sleep had become increasingly rare.

Selling Art

William Price and Thomas Werner had been doing an inventory of new paintings by Jimmy Snakespirit. William Price had returned from a trip to Louisiana with dozens of them and had spent only five hundred dollars for the lot. He was pleased to hear his partners calculation of their retail value.

"This gives us almost a hundred thousand dollars in inventory. We've got several people on the waiting list who are anxious to buy. You should have bought more…I mean, our costs will be met on the first sale."

"It's all he had." William Price repeated, having already explained that he'd bought everything that was available. "And this collection includes a few of what he calls the bad luck paintings…apparently he agrees that they're good and isn't totally convinced that they are evil, as his grandmother and mother tell him.

"It's amazing that they destroy them…" Thomas Werner nodded. "I mean, it's like burning money."

"Well, the grandma is really quite a witch. She insists that he does it and everyone in the village seems to do her bidding. The mother is quite a trip as well…" William Price picked up one of the paintings, examining it as he spoke. "When I was there,

Wanda Snakespirit's lover came to visit. He's a lounge singer. They make quite a couple."

"Well, there are all types in the world." Thomas Werner nodded his head in agreement.

William Price thought about Jimmy Snakespirit. Oddly, he found him attractive. Usually he preferred very pale young men. Yet, he knew that this wasn't just a physical attraction. Jimmy was an interesting man and, although Price discounted all of his voodoo beliefs, he found him to be quite mysterious. Buying and selling Jimmy's art was his business however and he never mixed his pleasure with it.

The Curse

Evil forces appeared in the paintings of Jimmy Snakespirit, along with angels. The people he knew and the woods he called home contained all of these spirits and his paintings encompassed all of this strange world. He had never entered a church, although he lived among people who built alters of saints in their living rooms. Jimmy always believed that there was no difference between God and nature and had little need for religion. Now, his world was falling apart and he sought an answer.

There was an artist named Reverend Howard Finster, who lived in Georgia. Jimmy had never met him, yet their work was often put in the same category; as being visionary and having mystical connections. Howard Finster claimed that God talked to him and his paintings were filled with religious messages. Not knowing where to turn, Jimmy considered that perhaps another artist, particularly one with a direct line to God could help him.

Jimmy drove north to the small town of Summerville, Georgia, where a gas station attendant gave him directions to the home of Howard Finster; a place called Paradise Garden. Once there, Jimmy parked his car by the side of the road and walked into this environment. He had never seen anything like it, yet he was comfortable there. When he was creating, Jimmy would actually feel that he was inside the painting and this place felt the same.

"Howard isn't here." A young man told him. "He's gone off to Washington D.C., to meet the president."

"Thanks." Jimmy said, turning to go. He stopped to look at a figure of an angel. As he stood there he understood. No one else could help him; not even an artist sent from God. He knew that no one could undo what he had done. He had sold the bad luck paintings and begun a series of events which could turn his gift into a curse. Soon, his life as an artist would be over.

Family Matters

"How you doing?" Brad's younger brother asked, making one of his rare phone calls home.

"Fine."

"And the family?"

"Everyone is doing fine." His brother was accustom to Brad being in denial and they both knew that he would at some point in the conversation dig deeper. "Have you seen our big brother lately?"

"Yeah, I drove down and visited him a couple of weeks ago. His wife is pregnant again, you know…"

"No, I didn't…Man, it's got to be a lot of work and really expensive raising those kids…"

When they were young, Brad was close to his brothers. When they became teenagers, they seemed to grow apart. Now they were like distant family. One taught college at a Southern University, and the other worked long hours as a blue collar worker to support his large family.

"How's mom?" He asked.

"The same." Brad said.

Brad's mother, Sarah Mitchell, remained beautiful. It was always apparent to him why his father married her. Yet, she had long been a danger to herself as well as the rest of the family;

forgetting to turn off the car after she's parked it in the garage, or baking cookies when the pilot had gone off in the stove.

"Do you think that she's suffering from depression?" Brad's brother asked.

"No Professor…" Brad answered. "I think that she's just sad."

"She's not suicidal, she's just forgetful." Dr. Katz would explain, after Sarah Mitchell or another family member were found in a deep and dangerous sleep. And Brad always believed that it was true. When he'd get angry with her for doing things like storing rat poison in an unmarked bell jar in the cupboard with the cereal and sugar, she always seemed so shocked.

Sarah Mitchell had always been one of the reasons that Brad couldn't leave his small town and family behind. Not only did she require some supervision, but she needed help in paying the bills. Of the little money Lenny Mitchell did make, much of it was spent during his travels. Gas, motel rooms, whiskey and women; living on the road could be quite expensive.

Many children believe that their parents don't have sex. For a time, when Brad was a child, and believed his family to be normal, his probably did. But for years they hadn't, at least not with each other. Lenny Mitchell always got his, but Sarah sat home and did without. She did have some sort of vibrator. It was an old device, that plugged into the wall. Brad took it away from her one day, when he saw her taking it out of the closet while running the bath. She hadn't smiled as much since that day, but he figured it better that she be alive than satisfied.

Lonely Brad

While many people feel very comfortable in a crowd and indeed fit in as a part of it, others feel very much set apart. For all of Brad's life, he felt even more alone in these situations than when he was sitting on the porch of his tree house, with only a book as his companion. He imagined that it might cease to be like this with time and it bothered him to realize that this was not ordinary. In an attempt to fit in, he sometimes went with friends for a drink at the Lamplighter or took the invitation to attend a party. He found himself watching more often than participating, always finding that people and their intentions were terribly transparent. It was obvious who had gone home with who, who regretted it and who would end up with who. He would thank the host or say his goodbyes and head home.

Socially, Brad had never really felt part of his home town, yet physically and emotionally, he had always felt connected. Knowing that he would never leave, he faced the reality that none of the girls from his home town were for him. What he believed in, was a theory of true love and destiny which he had gotten from watching old Hollywood movies with his mother and Aunt Jane. Many of the local girls were wonderful people; some were very sweet and others were very attractive. The girl of his dreams was not among them however. As the years past, he was beginning to suspect that he might never find her.

Another Night at Work

Brad and Tim were making pizza. Tim had flour on his face and pizza sauce on his shirt, but he was working hard and seemed happy. The telephone rang and Brad went to answer it.

"Hello, The Pizzeria." He answered.

"Hi Brad." It was Sarah Mitchell.

"Hi mom."

"Your father came home. He says that he's in the mood for one of your famous meatball sandwiches." She explained. "Would it be possible for you to make him one and deliver it?"

"Um…" Brad turned and looked at Tim, who spun a pizza dough into the air and failed to catch it. He turned back away, not wanting Tim to notice that he noticed.

"It will give the two of you an opportunity to have a nice talk." She explained.

"Sure mom." Brad hung up the phone and turned to Tim. "I need to run home and drop off a sandwich."

"But, don't you live thirty miles out of town?"

"Yeah, but I'll be back in an hour or so. I'm not worried…you'll be okay. I think that you're really getting the hang of things."

"Really? Do you think so?" Tim went to wipe some of the flour off of his cheek, but instead smeared pizza sauce on it.

"Sure." Brad told him.

Over the last decade, Brad hadn't seen much of his father, the one who he really needed to take care of the family. Lenny Mitchell had his career, which had always meant a lot to him; playing piano and singing in nightclubs. It didn't pay a lot of money, but it was his great love in life. He traveled to different towns, playing a week-end here and a week-end there. He earned enough extra income to make this life work by selling cleaning supplies (detergents and brushes) door to door. Lenny Mitchell always told Brad that they were the only normal ones in the family and that his staying at home for only short periods of time was the only way to maintain his sanity.

"You and I...we're the only normal ones in the family." Lenny Mitchell would tell his son, as often as not adding, "The only problem is...I'm not so sure about you."

Lenny always found this very amusing, and it caused him to laugh like a madman, which would lead to Brad's saying, "And I'm not so sure about you."

Lenny often laughed when his son said this, though not as much. In the North Woods, the residents often repeated conversations, until they got the timing right. They were like long complex cliches. It seemed that people found comfort in the way it added continuity to life.

When his father was home he would often sit on the back porch drinking. Mother would leave him alone when he was like this, explaining that he was lost in nostalgia; remembering times and dreams which had passed.

Maybe This is Love

Charlie bought a couple of beers at the market after work and pulled over in front of the Robert's place to drink them. He wanted to have a talk with Cyndi, but didn't have any idea what to say. He wanted her to know how serious he was about their being together. He wanted to know that he was the only man in her life and that he wanted it to remain that way. He didn't know how she saw the whole thing and wished he could know exactly what she was thinking. He didn't want to say that he was giving up his running around and drinking. He didn't want to make any promises. He certainly wasn't going to tell her that he loved her. The truth was that he was scared to death, because this indeed seemed to be the case.

How was he to know what love was about?

A North Wood's Evening

Marcia and Cyndi were sitting on the back porch, drinking beer and looking out at the cornfield.

"So this is what you do every evening?" Marcia wasn't complaining. It was all very pleasant. "It's just that I was wondering...this has been the way we've passed every evening since I came home."

"Did you want to go into town and have a drink or something?" Cyndi asked, taking a long slow drink from her beer.

"No, that's okay." Marcia told her. "This is fine."

It seemed odd to Marcia that her little sister didn't have more of a social life. She was, after all, young, single and beautiful.

Marcia Roberts had never really known her mother, who had died giving birth to Cyndi. She had some memories, enhanced by old family photos, but that was all. She didn't know her father terribly well either, aside from the fact that she was not impressed with him. It seemed to her a blessing that she had been sent off to school and she suspected that the social worker who had arranged it hadn't been impressed with him either. Although she was no doubt a very intelligent child, Marcia sometimes wondered if her being sent away didn't have more to do with the social worker's interest in getting her out of the bad environment, as her being gifted.

She was sorry that Cyndi had been left behind. To be raised by such a backward man, without a mother couldn't have been easy. Having an older sister around would certainly have been a help. Marcia had learned long ago that she shouldn't feel any guilt about the situation, as it wouldn't do her any good. She no longer saw a therapist, although she had for a few years in New York City, when she had suddenly been overtaken by anxiety attacks. She hadn't been aware of any feelings of confusion, guilt or doubt or self worth, yet they had apparently been there and needed to be done away with.

Now, she hoped to do something to help her sister, to make up for not being there all of those years.

Charlie was outside Cyndi's bedroom window. She had been sitting on the back porch, talking to her sister, for some time. Now, he heard them come back in the house. Her father was inside as well, watching television. Cyndi walked into her bedroom and Charlie knocked on the window. She quietly opened the window, leaning out and kissing him.

"Can you come out and play?" He asked.

"Sure. Go out to the barn. I'll meet you there."

"I don't think so." Charlie turned to see Mr. Roberts standing a few feet away, holding a shotgun.

"Uh, hello Mr. Roberts…"

"Cyndi, get back inside and shut that window."

"But Daddy…"

"Do as you're told girl."

Cyndi did as she was told, leaving Charlie standing alone, facing her father.

"Mr. Roberts, I want for you to know that my intentions are honorable…"

"Well, it seems to me that you're a married man."

"Only for the time being, sir. We're separated…and I want to do right by your daughter…"

"Well, I'll tell you what son…When I hear that you've been properly divorced from your wife and if I learn that you've got the money to support my girl after you're taken through the ringer and paying alimony and child support, then you can come calling."

"Yes sir." Charlie said, as he backed away. "Thank you."

"Thank you, son…"

An Evening at the Mitchell House

Aunt Jane was sitting in front of the television, reading a romance novel. Tina sat on the floor, playing with the baby.

"As we all know, the paintings of Southern primitive artist Jimmy Snakespirit, the so called *bad luck* paintings, have reportedly been responsible for over a dozen deaths among East Coast art collectors." It was one of the hosts of the prime-time tabloid show they always watched who was speaking. "The latest victim is reported to have been killed in a freak accident, when he opened the window in his thirteenth floor apartment and the breeze caused a painting to blow off the wall and across the room. He was hit in the head, causing him to fall out of the window to his death."

"Wow, truth is stranger than fiction." Tina said.

"Truth is based on fiction." Aunt Jane countered.

"You think so?" Tina asked, although she doubted that Aunt Jane knew any difference between the two.

"Sure…" Aunt Jane explained. "My life is based on those movies from the thirties…"

"They were called screwball comedies." Lenny Mitchell said, walking into the room.

"Yes." Aunt Jane nodded. "The movies were so much better in those days."

"Hello all…" Brad said, arriving home with the meatball sandwich for his father.

"Hello son." Lenny Mitchell said.

"I'll see if this needs to be heated up a bit." Sarah Mitchell came over and took the sandwich.

"I'm sure it's fine." Lenny said, offering her a smile and taking the sandwich.

Brad looked over at Tina and Aunt Jane and smiled at the baby, who smiled back and slobbered. He walked with his father through the room and out onto the back porch.

"Can I get the two of you a beer?" Sarah called out after them.

"Sure." They answered.

Brad and his father sat down on lawn chairs. His mother came out with two beers as well as a plate, knife and fork for her husband.

"Thanks hon." Lenny Mitchell said, unwrapping his sandwich.

"Well, I'll leave you two alone now, so that you can visit a bit." Sarah smiled and made her exit.

"Well, how's everything going, son?" Lenny Mitchell asked, before taking a bite of his sandwich.

"Okay, I guess. Things have been a little tough financially. There have been some bills for the house that had to be paid. Charlie pays his share, but refuses to pay for Tina and the baby. She works hard and makes some money, but she has a lot of expenses. Aunt Jane spends all of her Social Security money on lingerie that no one wants to see her wear.

"She was an attractive woman when she was younger, but she was always a little unbalanced."

"Most of my paycheck has been going toward taking care of things here."

"You don't know how well you have things, son. Do you know how many men your age have their own home, paid in full?"

"I live in a treehouse."

"Yeah, but you're happy right? I mean, it's what you've always wanted…"

"Yeah, but that's not the problem."

"You know that I bring home as much as I can Brad…You know that life on the road can be very expensive…"

"Can't you cut down on your expenses?"

"Well, I don't know…there's gas and motel rooms and, of course, just as it is here at home, there's the cost of food and drink…and, well, you know."

Brad felt that the "you know" was taking up the lion's share of the cost of his father's life on the road. He had long suspected that his father might be fooling around with other women and incurring their expenses in his travels. Yet, Brad was never fully able to believe this of his father.

"I worry about mom sometimes." Brad said, after a moment.

"No need to son. Your mother is a saint. God will watch out for her."

When Brad returned to The Pizzeria he found a young girl behind the counter, kissing Tim. She realized that she shouldn't be there with him and, embarrassed, left.

"I'm impressed." Brad told the grinning Tim.

"That's Susan, my girlfriend."

"She's cute."

"Do you have a girlfriend?"

"Not at the moment, but I've been meaning to get myself one." Tim nodded.

"Can I ask you a personal question?"

"Sure."

"You won't get mad?"

"Not at all. What is it?"

"Is it true that you can communicate with the dead?"

"Excuse me?"

"It's a rumor that I heard. My sister works at the apparel store and heard from your Aunt Jane that you had a gift for communicating with the dead."

"And that doesn't sound too bizarre to be true to you?"

"Well, yeah, kinda…"

"After all, my Aunt Jane is a little unbalanced."

"Yeah. I've heard that too."

A Visit from Marcia

One day, Marcia showed up on the Mitchell family's doorstep. Brad had been feeling that he wanted to know her better, but knew that he would always be afraid to approach her. When she arrived Brad was making his way down the hill, out of the woods, to the house. Sarah Mitchell and Aunt Jane were watching an old movie on television and had invited her to join them. Brad walked in the back door and through the kitchen to find them all sitting in the living room talking and watching the movie.

"Oh, I love this movie…" Marcia was saying. "Claudette Colbert was so wonderful."

"Yes…she was so pretty." Aunt Jane added. "When I was younger, I was quite attractive myself."

"Oh, you still are." Marcia said, looking up to see Brad standing there.

"Why thank you dear." Aunt Jane smiled. "Would you like to go shopping one day?"

Marcia nodded and smiled and got up.

"I wanted to talk with Brad about something." She said.

Brad and Marcia walked outside. She was wearing that baseball cap again, this time with a bra evident under her tee shirt, and blue jean cutoffs. For a New York Girl, he found that she blended very easily into the North Woods.

"Don't tell me that Charlie has been over at your place again..." Brad could see it on her face.

"Yes, and I came to warn you. I'm only responsible for her during the day. At night my father is home, and he keeps his shotgun propped up against the television."

"Wow." He said, thinking how symbolic it was, with all of the violence on television. "My family is odd, but yours is dangerous."

"Daddy is...and I wanted to let you know." She started to walk away, then stopped and turned. "By the way...I find your family to be very nice."

"Well, thank you."

Tina and the baby pulled into the drive then.

"This is Charlie's wife Tina and their baby." Brad told Marcia, as Tina got out and walked around to unstrap the baby from her seat.

"Hi." Tina said.

"This is Marcia Roberts." Brad announced.

"Oh, you're Cyndi's sister...Poor girl, I hear that Charlie really has it bad for her."

"Well, it seems to be the case, and I would suggest that you have a talk with him about it." Marcia was very serious, but very nice. She seemed to Brad to be genuinely concerned.

"Oh, I refuse to talk to him. I hate his guts."

Marcia looked at Brad and he shrugged.

"Have your dad shoot him." Tina went on. "That'll take care of the problem and get us some benefits."

Tina started toward the house, then turned and smiled.

"I don't really mean that." She explained. "I wish him well...I just wish that someone else wanted him."

She turned and went into the house.

"I like her." Marcia said, after a moment.

"Me too." Brad said. He hesitated, then decided to go ahead and say it. "And I want for you to know that, although you don't seem to think much of me, I um,…" he was stammering, not at all good at this type of thing. "I feel bad about all this trouble, but I'm glad that I met you."

Marcia smiled and nodded and said nothing for a moment.

"You seem like a good guy." She said finally.

And that was important to Brad, to be considered a good guy.

Marcia and Brad stood in the driveway and talked for a half hour. What they said wasn't really important; she told him a bit about her family and he told her something about his. What mattered was that they were passing time looking at each other and smiling. He said something funny and she laughed and gave him a look suggesting that he was witty. He said something stupid, and she gave him a look suggesting that he was an idiot. He made her laugh again and she smiled at him and looked at him in a good way. Brad decided that it was best to stop there. He told her that he was glad she stopped by and that they had talked. He didn't really want for her to leave, but didn't want to take the chance of having something happen that would cause her to leave with a bad impression of him.

"I'll say goodbye to your family." She said, walking up to the front door and poking her head in.

Brad followed behind her.

"Nice to meet you all." Marcia said.

Brad could hear his mother or Aunt Jane saying something to her. She stepped inside and he followed her in. Sarah Mitchell and Aunt Jane were still sitting on the sofa watching the movie. The baby was sitting in her crib, throwing toys out of it. Tina was stirring a bowl of cookie dough.

"Wanna stay for cookies?" She asked Marcia.

"No thanks…if I do I won't be hungry for dinner." Marcia said.

"We have the answer for that." Tina said. "We're having cookies for dinner."

"Come sit with us…it's almost the end of the movie." Sarah Mitchell said. "Just when you're ready to cry, there is a happy ending. I hate it when they do that. The couple is kissing and smiling and you find yourself crying your eyes out. Come and cry with us."

Marcia went over and sat down. Tina gestured for Brad to follow her into the kitchen.

Marcia, Sarah Mitchell and Aunt Jane were all instantly engrossed in the movie, so he went with Tina.

"You like her, don't you." She said, turning on the oven.

"Yeah I do."

"Just think…you could end up with her, Charlie could end up with Cyndi, I could find a nice guy…and it would be a happy ending."

"Yes." Brad said. He heard the ladies applauding in the other room.

Brad walked in to the room to find the credits rolling on the screen and the three of them in tears. He hated seeing his mother cry, although she did seem happy about it. He was as accustom to seeing Aunt Jane cry as he was to seeing her laugh, jump in the air and scream. She was always very emotional. It felt very strange seeing Marcia sitting there crying. Brad felt like going over and taking her in his arms, but realized that would be terribly forward.

Sarah Mitchell got up and turned off the television. Aunt Jane turned to Marcia and patted her on the leg.

"So…" She said. "Are you Brad's new girlfriend?"

"Uh, no…" Marcia said, turning and looking at Brad. "But we are friends."

"So you're a girl and he's a boy." Aunt Jane went on. "If you're his friend, then you're his girlfriend."

"Yes, well, I suppose in that context I am."

"Brad is very gifted you know." Sarah Mitchell said, sitting back down and smiling at him, to show how proud she was. Brad knew what she was getting at and went to say something to break into the conversation or change the subject. He was too late.

"Yes, he has a gift." Aunt Jane explained. "He can talk to the dead."

Marcia seemed to take it pretty well. She smiled at Sarah Mitchell and Aunt Jane and explained that she had to go.

"I'll see you around." She said to Brad, before going out the door.

Brad decided not to follow her. He wanted to yell at Mother and Aunt Jane, but knew that he wouldn't. They didn't realize that it was bad etiquette to tell the girl that he was falling in love with that he had a gift for talking to the dead. They didn't mean to cause any harm. After all...it was the truth.

Sad Little Girl

It was an ordinary afternoon. The television was tuned to a syndicated tabloid show, although no one was watching it. Again, it was about the artist Jimmy Snakespirit and how he had managed to elude the press and maintain his privacy. Aunt Jane sat in front of the television, reading a romance novel. Mother was in the kitchen, baking a pie, as Tina fed the baby.

Brad took a beer from the refrigerator and stopped in the living room to address Aunt Jane.

"Aunt Jane?…"

"Yes, Brad dear?…"

"I wish that you wouldn't tell people in town that I can talk to the dead."

"Oh, I'm sorry dear."

"I would appreciate it."

"Certainly dear."

Brad found Charlie in the garage, turning a bowl on his lathe. He was pressing a gouge against the outside of it and wood was flying every direction. He saw Brad and stopped. He set down his gouge and turned off the motor.

"Hey." Charlie said.

"How's it going?"

"Okay."

"Marcia was over." Brad told him, as he leaned against the work bench and took a long drink from his beer.

"Cyndi's sister? When?"

"Yesterday."

"How come?" He asked.

"She wanted to warn you about her father...That he might shoot you if he caught you coming around."

"Yeah, I know about her father." Charlie brushed off the bowl with his hand. "What do you think?"

"Looks nice." Brad nodded. "What kind of wood is it?"

"It's birch, from that big tree that was struck by lightening out by the Foster place."

"What are you going to do with all these bowls you've been making?"

"I don't know. I might be able to sell them. You know, there's that place that sells handmade crafts out on the highway."

"You've talked to them?"

"No. Cyndi mentioned it though. She likes art. See these candlesticks?" Charlie walked over to the work bench and picked them up. They had been painted in bold colors. "I turned these the other day and Cyndi painted them. She figures that maybe someday we can make all sorts of things and sell them there."

"I guess it's possible."

Charlie stood there for a moment, holding the candlesticks and looking past them.

"Sometimes she cries..." He said finally. "...For no damn reason at all."

It had been important to Charlie that Brad meet Cyndi. Now it was important that he know more about her. Brad had never seen such a serious expression on his cousin's face.

"She must be crying for some reason." Brad told him. "It might seem something trivial, not worth crying about, but it's got to be something."

"Yeah, it's always something, but it can be anything. One time she said that she was worried that I loved her too much...hell, I do love her. I love her a lot. But too much? Why would she think that? And why would she think that it's a problem?"

"I don't know. Maybe she's worried that the two of you are getting too close or moving too fast..."

"No, that's not it. If a day passes and I don't call her, she cries because she's worried that I wasn't ever going to call her again."

"Well, I guess that she's just moody." Brad wished that it was his father Charlie was talking to. Lenny Mitchell always had an opinion on women and would be happy to offer advice. Brad wondered what his father would say; if he would tell Charlie that women were always sad or confused.

"I mean, I'm used to my mom and your mom crying. It's not really a big deal. And Tina used to cry, back before she took to yelling at me instead. It's never meant much to me...I mean, it just about breaks my heart when Cyndi cries. You know, for her to be so sad..."

Charlie wasn't the type of man to discuss his feelings and he and Brad had certainly never had a heart to heart conversation. Brad listened to him and tried to help. Due to his lack of experience, he had little advice to offer. Brad left and Charlie went back to turning wood and thinking it all over.

Marcia Goes to Town

Marcia Roberts pulled into town and parked her car. She started up the street and entered the lingerie shop. Mary was standing outside, smoking a cigarette.

"Hello." Mary said, smiling and following her in. "Can I help you find anything?"

"Just looking for now, thanks."

"Well, let me know." Mary said, turning and approaching one of the other salesgirls. "You know..." Marcia heard her say. "That Brad sure is cute."

"Why don't you ask him out. You've waited long enough for him to ask you." The salesgirl was chewing gum and working on a display of flowery panties.

"I can't tell if he likes me." Mary shrugged.

"Men don't know what they like." The salesgirl said with a roll of the eyes and two shakes of the head. "If you want him, you've got to make him want you..."

The salesgirl picked up a lacy piece of lingerie, holding it up to Mary.

"Something like that would do the job." Another salesgirl offered.

"You two are such good salesgirls..." Mary said, giggling. "But what am I supposed to do?...Walk in off the street, wearing just this and order a pizza?"

The girls laughed and Marcia went to exit.

"Thanks." Marcia said, going out the door.

"Come back again." Mary called out after her.

"I think I might." Marcia said, not loud enough for them to hear, once she was out on the street.

She noticed the sign for the pizzeria, paused and walked inside. Tim was standing behind the counter.

"Hi." He smiled, quite happy to be setting up the kitchen. "We're not open yet."

"Does Brad Mitchell work here?"

"Yeah, he's in the back. Hey Brad!...someone is here to see you!"

Brad was in the back, doing prep work. He hated cutting onions, but it was something which needed to be done. He had considered having Tim do them, but wasn't sure he should. For one, it was a terrible job and very hard on the eyes and he thought it wrong to stick the new guy with it. Also, Brad was concerned that Tim wasn't terribly coordinated and was concerned that he might cut himself. Brad heard Tim call for him and walked out front, surprised to see Marcia standing there.

"Oh, hi..."

"Hi. I was just down at the lingerie store and this girl, with the hots for you, mentioned that you worked here."

"That was probably my sister Mary." Tim volunteered.

"Oh, I'm sorry." Marcia said, embarrassed.

"That's okay, it's true." Tim shrugged and continued with his work.

"Your sister has the hots for me?" Brad asked him.

"You didn't know that?" Tim asked.

"If she listens to her friend's advice, everyone will know it." Marcia said, looking at Brad as though he was up to no good.

"Gosh, all those nights spent alone, not knowing…" Brad smiled, thinking that he was being funny. Fact was, he'd suspected that he had a chance with Mary, but had never been interested.

"Well, I guess I'll go." Marcia said, not appearing to be particularly impressed.

"Wait a minute…you stopped by just to tell me that?" Brad asked.

"Oh no, I really just stopped by to say hello." She had turned and started toward the door.

"Listen, I'd like to explain about, you know, what my family said." Brad wanted to explain, but had no idea how to.

"About you being very gifted?" Marcia turned and looked at him and continued to walk backward toward the door.

"Yes, that."

"You don't need to." Marcia said, opening the door and starting out.

"But I want to." Brad realized that he sounded a little desperate, which he was.

"I'll see you." Marcia said, pausing in the doorway. She smiled at him, which suggested that it was alright.

Brad stood there a moment after she was gone. He told himself that she liked him a little bit and that he still had a chance with her. He would wait a few days, which he knew would be tough, then give her a call. Brad knew that he was terribly attracted to Marcia Roberts and that he had to be brave.

Concern About the Gift

For a time, when Brad was in his early teens, he suspected that he needed to see a psychiatrist. He knew that being visited by the dead each time he came into contact with their handwriting was far from normal and he feared that he was suffering from a terrible mental illness. There were certainly indications that it ran in the family. He wasn't sure how to proceed and didn't want for everyone to know about it. He knew that the one person a young man could trust was his mother and one day asked her to go for a walk with him. Once they were far off on their own, he told her.

"Mom…I think there may be something wrong with me."

"Oh, I doubt it very much. You're just going through adolescence…becoming a man. Didn't your father have a talk with you about that?"

"No, that's not it. There's something else…"

"Oh. Well, what is it dear?"

"I've been having hallucinations or something…seeing the dead."

"Oh." They walked and said nothing for a while. "The dead?"

"Yes. The dead."

"I see."

It was apparent to him that his mother didn't know what to say. They continued down the road, neither of them saying a word. Lenny Mitchell, who had gone into town for beer, drove up over the hill. He pulled up and stopped the car.

"What's up?" He asked.

"Brad is unhappy and it's all your fault." Sarah Mitchell told him.

"What is it son?" He asked.

Brad didn't really want to talk to his father. He figured that his mother would understand, having a sister like Jane and all, and that she would perhaps comfort him and tell him that it was a stage that everyone in the family went through. He figured that his father, who was always commenting on the madness on his wife's side of the family, would probably have no appreciation or understanding of the situation.

"It's nothing." Brad told his father.

"It's nothing that was a problem before you went and got him involved with those people." Sarah Mitchell told her husband.

Brad wasn't certain that he heard her right. He had no idea what she was talking about.

"You two want a ride back to the house?" Lenny Mitchell asked.

"No." She stepped back away from his car and turned away. Lenny Mitchell looked at Brad and shrugged his shoulders, then continued on his way home.

"I always knew that you would be very gifted." Sarah Mitchell told Brad as they walked back toward the house.

"Seems more like a curse." Brad told her. "It's scary."

"I'm sure that you'll grow accustomed to it." She said with a forced smile. "I'm sure that you have this ability for a reason and that one day you'll understand it."

It was apparent to Brad that, while his mother was trying to be very reassuring, she was in fact concerned and angry with her husband. Once they got home, she insisted on having a talk with Lenny Mitchell and led him into the bedroom where they spoke at length in hushed tones. Brad went up the trail to his tree house, where he once again passed the hours trying to understand his life and finding it baffling.

Green Hills Road

There was a road off the highway, a half mile north of the Pancake House. When Brad was growing up, they called it Old Cemetery Road, although there was no sign. It's actual name remained what it had been for over a century, simply Cemetery. More recently a group of real estate developers had bought property along the road and had it's name changed to Green Hills Road. The cemetery was three miles down the road and over a hill. There seemed no reason why people shouldn't build homes on this beautiful tree lined road, once the addresses no longer read like cemetery plots.

The people residing at the end of the road had for some time outnumbered those who lived in town. The cemetery contained a wide variety of tomb stones, from large statues placed to announce those who were wealthy, to small rocks which represented those who could not afford a permanent marker. Several of the residents lived through the Revolutionary War and a number of them fought in the Civil War. Most believed in God and included a verse or symbol on their stones to make this known. It was said that the place had been an Indian burial ground, although no physical evidence of this was ever found.

Mr. Ellison would walk past the prefabricated homes on Green Hills Road on his way to visit the cemetery. Not only did he have friends and family who were buried there, but he knew the histories and genealogies of almost every resident. Brad would often accompany Mr. Ellison on his visits, although he wasn't up to the walk and would drive out there with him. They would walk past the tombstones and Mr. Ellison would tell him anecdotes about the people. He would say, "Oh, you know this person" and sure enough it would be someone Brad had used his gift to converse with. Brad felt great respect for the people who were buried there and felt somehow indebted to them. Although very few of them were actually related to him, they were people who had worked hard and made it possible for him to enjoy life in his home town.

Brad had felt this way long before Mr. Ellison introduced him to his old friends. The cemetery was a place to go drinking with some of his classmates and from the beginning Brad had felt that this was wrong. It seemed to him that living and having fun was not an insult to the deceased, but people often ended up shattering beer bottles against the tombstones or urinating on them. By this time, Brad was aware that the dead lived on and he worried that they were aware of this. Even if this was not the case, it seemed disrespectful.

"Ah, you take this little town too seriously." Randy would say, although Brad eventually convinced him that the cemetery was not a good place to party. "In the larger scheme of things, these people and this place are not important.

"I think that they are." Brad countered. "I think that places and people are all that really matter."

This never made any sense to Randy and Brad knew that he could never explain it to him. Yet this belief was a driving force in his life, keeping him home and causing him to be as respectful as possible to the people he met.

"Don't you ever want to be bad?...Really bad?" Susan Fisher asked Brad one night, as she, Randy and Brad sat on the hill behind the cemetery, drinking whiskey. "They say that good guys finish last...that good girls go to heaven, but that bad girls go everywhere."

"Who says that?" Brad asked.

"My dad told me the first one and I saw the second on a bumpersticker." She explained.

"Cool is the rule..." Randy offered. "...But sometimes bad is bad."

Randy and Susan looked at each other for a moment, their cliches having made them feel very passionate, then got up and walked away together. They disappeared into a group of trees and Brad was left alone there, looking down at the cemetery.

"Why do you think that I've lived so long?" Mr. Ellison asked Brad one day, as they sat on the old wood fence which surrounded the cemetery.

"You told me that it was drinking burgundy and eating chocolate everyday." Brad offered.

"Not how, but why?" He asked. It was apparent that he was suddenly feeling very melancholy. It often happened and at these times he wanted to talk and he didn't want to be cheered up.

"What do you think?" Brad asked him.

"I was wondering if you knew." Mr. Ellison answered. Brad had no idea why it was or what he expected him to say. It appeared to be a riddle or quiz. Mr. Ellison liked to believe that Brad was very sharp and Brad enjoyed proving him right.

Brad had always known Mr. Ellison, but it hadn't occurred to him that he should get to know the old man when he was growing up. Brad had stopped by the Historical Society once and had got to chatting with him and playing a game of chess when he was in high school. Soon after, Brad made a habit of it. It wasn't clear whether Brad was an old soul or if Mr. Ellison was eternally youthful, but they got along very well.

If Mr. Ellison had passed on back when his contemporaries had, Brad's life would have been different. He would not have spent time at the Historical Society and come to know the Hotel Magnificent and all of the celebrities and characters who visited and lived in Odinville. He would not have known their stories and perhaps would never have taken advantage of his gift.

"I know that if you hadn't lived so long, I would have never come to know all I do about my corner of the world." Brad said.

"It's not just a corner of the world." Mr. Ellison said, standing up slowly and allowing his legs to creak and adjust. He looked at the cemetery for a moment, then turned and started toward the car. "It's the center of the Universe."

A Visit from Smith

Marcia Roberts awoke in Thomas' apartment. She climbed to her feet and found her way through the familiar darkness to the door. It was night, but a full moon was in the sky, illuminating the main room. The lights of New York City were bright as well, and colors cascaded from them across the white carpet. She saw Thomas sitting in his large overstuffed chair, with an empty wine glass in his hand.

"Well, you're back now." He said, with a smirk and victorious nodding of the head. "You can get me a refill."

Marcia nodded, and took the glass from him. He grabbed her hand, and held her there with him.

"You were smart to come back..." He told her. "How could there have been anything there for you? Here you help to publish books...and books create minds...and minds create worlds."

"I suppose that you think even God reads books?" She hissed, not happy to be back. She pulled away from Thomas, and started toward the kitchen.

"Well, if he existed he would be here in New York, working in the publishing business. I mean, do you know how much money there is being made in Bible publishing?..."

"I think that God is an artist." She said absently, as she left the room.

"Well then, he would publish a coffee table book." Thomas shouted after her.

The kitchen window shades were drawn and she reached out to turn on the light. She was surprised to see Smith sitting at the kitchen table. She wasn't unhappy to see him, as she'd always thought he was a very nice man. It did bother her however, that he had been dead for a number of years. She remained calm, smiling and greeting him.

"He needs you more than you need him." Smith said.

"I know."

"The same is true of this entire town…You should go out on your own. Publish the kind of book that you believe in."

"It's very expensive to start a publishing house, even a small one." Marcia offered, opening the refrigerator door, and taking out the bottle of Chardonnay. "Would you like a glass of wine?"

"No thanks." Smith looked good for a dead man, not discolored or unhealthy. "All the money you'll need to get started is out in the cornfield."

"I know." She said.

She realized then why she was so calm, and why Smith was able to be there with her. Since she'd come to the North Woods she'd been dreaming quite a bit and suddenly dreaming in color. She slept peacefully, happy to know that she hadn't gone back to Thomas in New York.

The Shoes

Brad wore his grandfather's shoes. He'd passed away when Brad was a child and the only memories Brad had of the old man was his Sunday visits when he would appear in his dark suit and shiny black shoes. Grandpa Mitchell would sit in the recliner, take a cloth from his coat pocket and wipe them down as soon as he walked into the house. It seemed a little odd to Brad, as a child who delighted in walking in the woods and getting dirty. Out of respect for his grandfather and his shoes, Brad came to treat the shoes with the same care.

Grandpa Mitchell had taught his children that if you bought good shoes and took care of them, they would last all your life. They didn't listen to him and took to purchasing cheap shoes, perhaps as an act of independence, and always having to replace them. The old man purchased his shoes from a small manufacturer in England and, when they weren't being worn, they were stored in their original boxes in the closet.

When Grandpa Mitchell died, this was where Lenny Mitchell found them. The old man was size ten and a half and Lenny Mitchell wore size twelve. All of the boys were young and their father figured that he should hold onto them and see if any of them turned out to be the same size. Grandpa Mitchell's affairs were put in order and most of his possessions were sold, given or thrown away. The boxes of shoes went into the attic.

Years later, as the family was finishing dinner, Lenny Mitchell went up to the attic and got the shoes. Brad's little brother was only thirteen, but his feet were almost as large as his fathers. Brad's older brother was size ten, but didn't even want to know if any of the shoes fit him. He said that it seemed to him sort of creepy to be walking around in one's dead grandfather's shoes. Being size ten and a half and having faint but fine memories of his grandfather, Brad was happy to have the shoes. He removed the black dress shoes from the box and put them on. Instinctively, he took a cloth from the box and wiped them off. The Mitchell family stood and stared, saying nothing. After a moment, Sarah Mitchell placed a pie on the table and they sat down for dessert.

"I knew your grandfather well." Mr. Ellison told Brad, years after he had started to wear the shoes. "He was a rather odd man, if you don't mind me saying so, but he was a good man. He was terribly religious—perhaps to the point of being fanatical. That's probably why we weren't all that close. No one likes a preacher."

"My dad says that he started his own church."

"Yes, he did." He was for the most part a Baptist, but he had certain beliefs that sort of set him apart. For one, he didn't believe that Heaven was a place off somewhere, where you went when you died. He was convinced that Heaven was more a spiritual manifestation, that existed on Earth but was eternal. He had all the Bible quotes necessary to prove it, but it seemed a rather revolutionary approach to most. The local congregation's preacher didn't really think much of it."

"Maybe he was the one who burnt down the church." Brad had heard that Grandpa Mitchell had built a chapel and had developed a congregation. Over a period of two decades, his church body slowly grew, until a mysterious fire destroyed the church. Grandpa Mitchell had never believed in taking money from parishioners, another revolutionary idea, and hadn't the capital to rebuild it. His spirit was broken and after the fire he gave it all up and went back to being a farmer.

"That would have been Reverend Jones and he would never have done such a thing. He was too good a man. Fact was, he and your grandfather were drinking buddies when they were younger. I have no idea who burned down your grandfather's church. He took it hard though and gave up the idea of having his own church. Lord knows that he didn't cease preaching though…"

This was the grandfather Brad had known as a child, the old preacher without a church. Brad never really knew the man, but went through life wearing his shoes.

Almost Home

They stopped at a motel, rather than driving all night to get home. Lenny Mitchell knew the man who owned it and they got their rooms at reduced rates. Once they had their keys, Lenny began to walk quietly away to his room, then turned to look at Brad and Marcia.

"I guess that we'll get up early and head out." He said.

Brad nodded.

Lenny Mitchell turned and went on his way. Brad watched him a moment, then turned to find Marcia watching him. As he took her by the hand and they walked to their room, he wondered how much a life is filled with moments of watching. After all, it was essentially all people did…A man watches a girl, then approaches her. They spend a period of time taking in each others actions and feelings. Perhaps they decide to get married and invite everyone they know to watch. And then they'll watch their children grow up and watch their live pass by.

Perhaps this was why people fell into watching television so easily. Brad had never had a television in his treehouse and now he knew why. Aside from the fact that it was in keeping with his living practically in another century, he had always enjoyed observing the people in his town and writing about them. Also, he was able to observe those who came before, being equipped with the ability to communicate with the dead. Not everyone had such built in entertainment centers.

Brad thought it was quite possible that he would start watching television, now that everything had changed. He would probably be much more of an ordinary guy.

Lenny Mitchell stretched out on the bed and thought about his wife. It came to his mind, how it had all started. Back then, he drove a 1948 Buick, a car that was almost ten years old, yet in mint condition and paid for. He had just graduated from high school and believed that he would soon leave Odinville and the North Woods far behind. He was destined to go off to the city, where he would find success. He played piano like Fats Domino and wore his hair like Jerry Lee Lewis. He could sing and he wrote songs. He could be another Elvis. There was only one reason for him to hesitate—to stay in town from day to day. He was in love and there wasn't a doubt in his mind that he would someday marry his beautiful Sarah. She wasn't prepared to run off with him and he couldn't bring himself to leave her behind. He knew that her mother and Uncle Sam were against him. If he gave them the space, they would do everything in their power to drive a wedge between them and fix her up with who they considered a better prospect.

Lenny and Sarah would go into Bay Springs almost every evening and drive down Main Street in his Buick. Sometimes they would stop at Henry's for hamburgers and shakes and sometimes they would just drive down to the waterfront, where they would sit and watch the waves hammer the breakwall. It was there, one July night, that they made love for the first time. And once they were lovers, they knew that they were committed to each other; that neither of them could ever leave the other. When Sarah learned that she was pregnant,

Lenny never considered anything other than living up to that commitment. He proposed to her and, considering the situation, her Mother and Uncle Sam begrudgingly agreed.

Lenny Mitchell got a job as a regional sales representative for a company that manufactured soaps and carried a line of brushes. They were reasonably priced and easy to sell to local housewives. He found that he could earn extra income by going door to door after he closed up shop. The income helped when Sarah discovered that she was pregnant for the second, then third time. Lenny didn't consider his dream dead; rather it was only postponed. He would play the piano in the evening or they would play cards and talk about the future.

Lenny Mitchell would regularly go out on tour. This meant that he was booked into a series of small clubs, to play for small change. He would also go door to door by day, peddling soaps and home products, one of the last of the traveling salesmen. This also meant motel rooms and being in bars until late at night. Before Wanda, he wasn't one to fool around. In fact he'd once started a Catholic Gospel Band. If they'd found success it would have perhaps kept him from this. Yet, he hadn't sought out this life. It had happened to him.

Evenings would find him on a barstool, talking with one of the bartenders he had befriended in his travels.

"Who was that number you left here with last night?" The bartender would ask.

"Charlene." He'd answer. "Or Cherie...Something like that..."

"Gonna see her again tonight?"

"No, I'm hitting the road right after the gig. I've got a lady down in Louisiana you know..."

"Yes." The bartender would grin. "Your voodoo woman."

"Yes." Lenny would echo. "My voodoo woman."

Lenny Mitchell saw himself as a man who was down on his luck, who did everything he could to make himself and those around him happy. When he learned that Sarah was pregnant, he hadn't hesitated to do the right thing. They were married and he put his plans for a musical career on hold and got himself a job. For years after they were married, he would often pull up to the highway in his Buick and just sit there for a time, staring down the road. He loved her so much, yet he never doubted that one day he would leave. His heart would break, but he would go off and find his destiny on the lonesome road.

When he left Sarah the first time, it was after an argument. Although he was convinced that he was out of her life for good as he slammed the door to the house behind him, within a few miles he was aware that he would go back. He left her many times after that, but he was always back, holding her and comforted by her arms again.

There was a time when Lenny and Sarah caused each other to burn in a way that led to a happiness beyond marital bliss. This was part of the reason he always came back, it was good love and good sex and he knew that most men didn't have it so good.

One night changed all this, the first time he was ever seduced. The first time he had desired another woman and allowed himself to feel his body pressed up against hers. Wanda Snakespirit was not just any woman and it was no ordinary night.

It was just a Week Earlier...

Brad was at the Historical Society, playing chess with Mr. Ellison. Preoccupied, not knowing how to go about approaching Marcia, he was playing badly. Mr. Ellison occasionally looked at him with concern, figuring that once he won the game, he'd ask what was on Brad's mind.

They saw a car pull into the parking lot, a relatively rare occurrence.

"Checkmate" Mr. Ellison said. Brad studied the board for a moment and knew that it was true.

"Good afternoon gentleman."

Brad turned to see Marcia standing in the doorway. He looked over at Mr. Ellison to see him watching his face. Brad supposed that his mouth must have been open, or his expression apparent.

"Good afternoon Miss Roberts." Mr. Ellison climbed to his feet.

"What have you found out about my great Uncle?"

She came in and Brad noticed that she was wearing the uniform of tourists; a polo shirt and a pair of brightly colored Bermuda shorts. Usually this outfit brought out the worst in a physique, accentuating skinny legs or a bulging torso. Marcia Roberts was the first person Brad had ever seen, who looked good dressed like this.

They shared a smile, as Mr. Ellison walked over and picked a file up off of the desk.

"Birth records. That's about it. Apparently he left town when he was young, and never came back."

"That's it, eh?" She seemed a bit disappointed. Mr. Ellison turned to look at Brad and smiled, a twinkle in his eye.

"That's all I could find. Brad is usually a great help with research, but he couldn't come up with anything either. Isn't that right Brad?"

Brad nodded his head.

"Sorry." He said.

"Listen Brad, can you watch the shop for a bit?" Mr. Ellison started toward the door. "I'm going over to the market to get some candy."

Brad appreciated the old man being sensitive to his wanting to be alone with Marcia, but he was a bit afraid. Mr. Ellison went out and Marcia walked over and sat at his place at the table.

"So…You help with research…Does this involve your gift?" She asked.

"I know how it sounds, but I would like for you to understand." She said nothing and sat looking at Brad, so he continued. "Do you believe in psychics…and that type of thing?"

"I believe that there are more things in heaven and earth, Horatio…and I'm willing to listen." Saying this she smiled at Brad and he felt much better. He felt as though he could go ahead and tell her all about the gift and that she wouldn't find him odd.

"Well, you know how most psychics say that if they hold someone's possession, they can tell something about them?…" He started.

"Go on."

"And you know how people who study handwriting analysis can examine someone's writing and know something about them?"

"Yes…but that's more of a science."

"Yes, well…you know how people have seances, and claim to be able to communicate with the dead?…"

"Yes…but you're talking about all sorts of various paranormal experience…"

"Well, my gift is sort of like each of those, but not really like any of them…" Brad paused. She was listening intently, and it seemed she cared and wanted to understand. "It's this…If I hold a piece of paper which someone has written on in my hands, I can communicate with that person. That is if the person is deceased."

"And you really believe that you have this talent…" She didn't speak as if she doubted it, but rather that she wanted clarification.

"Yes."

"Wait here for a moment." Marcia said, getting up and going out to her car.

Brad felt good that she didn't say that he was crazy and stomp out. "Wait here" sounded so inviting. Yet he listened, half expecting to hear the sound of her starting her car and pulling out of the parking lot. Marcia came back in with two pieces of paper with handwriting on them, handing him one. It was apparently a test and he felt very good about that. She was giving him a chance to prove to her quickly and easily that he wasn't crazy…that he in fact had quite an impressive gift. Once one got over the fact that it was very odd, that is.

Brad held the first piece of paper in his hands and closed his eyes. He felt nothing. Brad opened his eyes and looked at Marcia and shrugged.

"This person must be still alive." He said.

"Yes." She nodded, smiled and handed him the other sheet. "Good."

"This man lived in a small cabin." The moment Brad touched the second piece of paper, there were images. "He owned a gun, which he kept propped up in the corner. But he seems friendly, not the type that would shoot someone without having a good reason. Ah, and he has a wife. She's very attractive…in fact she looks quite a bit like you." He handed the piece of paper back to her. "I've got it…it's your Grandma and Grandpa."

"You haven't proven anything yet…" She held the piece of paper out. "You said that you can communicate with them."

"Do you promise that they are nice people? I hate getting into the heads of dead people who are angry or violent…"

"No, they're very sweet. I want for you to ask them questions. If you get the correct answers, I'll believe in your gift."

"Okay." Brad said, accepting the challenge, willing to do anything for love.

He had a short talk with them, then handed her back the letter.

"They say that they were married on Valentines Day, that they had two children and that they both died the year of their fiftieth wedding anniversary. They say that they're still together and they love each other."

Marcia looked stunned, then she smiled, her eyes filling with water.

"And they are very sweet aren't they?" She asked.

Brad nodded. She handed the letter back to him.

"Ask them if the story about my Great Uncle Claude robbing a bank and burying the money on our property is true."

Brad hesitated and remembered something she'd said that first day, about buried treasure. It suddenly became apparent that she needed him and he realized that he could benefit from that.

"I will if you go out with me tonight." He said, handing the letter back.

"Okay." She took the letter, looked at it and nodded. "I'll tell you what…I'll bring the letter and we'll do it over dinner."

"Sounds romantic." Brad said.

"And if it is true, dinner is on me." She offered.

"Fair enough."

Brad walked out onto the porch with her. She went to her car and got in. They waved at each other as she drove away.

"Man…" He told himself. "She is really impressed with me."

Songs and Love

Driving home, Brad listened to the tape of songs Randy had recorded in Los Angeles. They had often talked about matters of the heart and Randy had never really taken to Brad's idea that the perfect girl for him would one day show up in town. Brad had never taken his friend's opinion regarding this too seriously, as Randy's relationships tended to be short and Brad found comfort in his sense of romantic destiny.

From Brad's conversations with Randy about Lorna, it seemed that his friend had eventually fallen in love. Brad found this somewhat comforting, as he felt that everyone should fall in love at least once before leaving the world. Randy didn't expect Brad to ever find his dream girl and Brad had never expected Randy to find his.

Lorna Petersen and Randy had met at the Vanilla Room, a Hollywood nightclub, during open mike night. She played a song she had written called *Looking at You in the Rearview Mirror*. Randy was scheduled to go on after her and he stopped her as she came off the stage, asking her if she could stay awhile. He explained that he wanted to talk to her and she smiled and nodded.

Randy played a song called *Goodbye*. He and Brad had written it together years before and they had always referred to it as

Randy's theme song. It was an anthem about failure to commit to relationships. He was hoping that he and Lorna might become lovers, yet felt it only fair to give her some indication of his way of life. She watched him and heard the words and afterward agreed to go back to his place for a beer. The next day he asked her to stay, a request he made of her a hundred times after that.

Lorna loved music, but had neither the commitment or talent that Randy did. They would sometimes play guitar in the evening, but usually they talked or made love and Randy's music was a world quite distinct from hers. Soon she stopped going to the recording studio with him, or to gigs. She knew that he might play a set at the Vanilla Room, then hurry home to her, but understood that he could as easily get involved in a jam session at the club which lasted deep into the night.

"So, what are you gonna' do tonight?" Randy asked her, placing his guitar in it's case.

"I brought some work home from the office." She said.

"I'm gonna play the songs that I've been recording." Randy told her. "They're the songs that Brad and I wrote together. I've put them in order, so that there is a definite story line…"

"Ah, so you're back to that idea again."

"Yeah, I figure it would make for a great concept album…"

"They're Brad's lyrics, right? And they tell the story of his life. What would he think?"

"Oh, he'll be jazzed. That is, as long as I don't expose his gift to the world. There's only one problem with the whole thing. I don't know how the story ends."

The Date

When Brad was thirteen, he made the decision to always wear blue jeans. For him, they represented America, rock n' roll and a commitment to be true to himself. He would allow only the smallest compromise; that on special occasions, such as a church wedding or an invitation from the White House, he would wear black jeans. Two decades later, his wardrobe consisted of a half dozen pairs of blue jeans, denim overalls and one pair of unworn, black jeans. Aside from a selection of t-shirts in a variety of colors, he had one white dress shirt. Dinner with Marcia Roberts seemed an occasion worthy of his finest apparel and Brad removed the black jeans and dinner jacket from his closet. He added a tie and a black dinner jacket, borrowed from his father's closet, and he set out.

He had made reservations at the Lamplighter, the nicest restaurant in the county, and picked Marcia up for dinner at seven o'clock. She walked out onto the porch when he pulled up and he got out and escorted her to the car. It was the first time Brad had seen her in a dress, and he took a long, slow look. The dress was simple, without a pattern, and reached from high above her cleavage to her knees. He wasn't certain why it seemed so sexy and considered that perhaps it had to do with him.

"Reservations are at eight." Brad told her, as they drove toward town. Every time he had met Marcia Roberts, he found myself more anxious to see her again. Now he was wanting very much to have her closer to him. "We can have a drink before dinner."

"Okay." She said, patting the purse which sat tight upon her lap. Brad knew that it was because the paper with her Grandfather's writing was in there and that she was preoccupied with suspense.

"If you want we can do the thing with the letter before dinner." He offered. "Otherwise, I'll feel like I'm holding out on you and forcing you to have dinner with me."

"Okay." She said.

As they drove, Brad looked over at her occasionally. It was dark and he would take advantage of every car that passed, turning to look at her with the benefit of their headlights. She was wearing short, gold, dangle earrings and a gold chain around her neck. She wore make-up and Brad found that he couldn't remember whether she had been wearing make-up the other times he'd seen her. If so, it was very light and natural at that time. Now her lips were red and her eye lashes were black.

It was a forty five minute drive into Bay Springs and Brad and Marcia hardly talked the entire way. He was nervous and she seemed uncomfortable.

"These rumors of buried treasure seem to invade our happiness." He thought, pulling into the Lamplighter parking lot. He told himself that with a couple of drinks, there would be good vibes between them.

Inside, there was the normal assortment of locals. You could tell the wealthy ones, because they wore golf shirts or green pants and sat in the dining room. In most cases it was a man and his wife, with very little conversation going on between them. Sometimes it was two couples, with a great deal of laughing and conversation going on. Occasionally it was two men, apparently discussing business, with good eye contact and sincere faces. The struggling working stiffs were drinking beer in the lounge. The ones who weren't staring at the game on the television screen were talking loud and laughing.

"The dining room is only half full." Brad said. "I guess I didn't need reservations."

"It's half empty." Marcia said. She glanced about and it was clear she didn't want to have a drink at the bar. "Maybe we can get a table now, and have a drink in there before dinner."

The hostess approached them.

"Hi Brad." She said.

"Hi." He said, with a smile and a nod, a little embarrassed. He knew her from school, although not well enough that he could remember her name. He was thrown by the way she acted; as though she knew him well.

"Would the two of you like to have drinks before dinner?"

Brad looked over at Marcia, who looked again at the crowded bar, full of locals and frowned.

"Maybe we'll have a drink at our table before dinner." Brad told her.

"Okay." The hostess took two menus, then spun about dramatically, walking ahead of them slowly. She was wearing a long tight dress, which showed off her rather attractive back side. She turned to see if Brad was looking at her, and Marcia looked to see if he was looking at her. He was, but was acting as though he wasn't.

The hostess sat them near the window, at a table which overlooked the docks. Handing them the menus, she gave Brad a rather odd, raised eyebrow look. "Enjoy your dinner." She said, then made her exit.

Brad had never eaten at the Lamplighter, even though he'd had drinks there many times. His lot was more like the guys in the bar, than the successful and retired that sat in the restaurant. Then again, he felt quite unlike any of them. Looking around, he imagined that his father probably took women to similar restaurants while on the road. He was a good salesman and he claimed to be making so little. Brad suspected that he was spending time selling himself and buying pleasure. It angered him to know that he was covering his father's expenses, and taking on his responsibilities. Brad knew where the money was going. He thought to himself that if the good life was good enough for his father, it was good enough for him. Yet Brad knew that he would never be one to stray, as his father had.

"So, do you know every girl in town?" Marcia asked, nodding the direction of the hostess.

"I went to school with her." He explained. "No one ever moves here, and you tend to know just about everyone who stays."

"Small town life." She said.

"It's fine, once you get used to it."

"Did you see Charlie?…" Marcia asked. "…In the bar…"

"No I didn't." Brad turned and looked back at the bar. There was Charlie with a mug in hand and a smile on his face. He was sitting at the end of the bar, looking at them.

"Why is he smiling?" She asked.

"I don't know…Just ignore him and he'll go away."

"I hope that he's not smiling because he thinks that Cyndi is home alone and unprotected just because I'm here. Daddy is home tonight and won't hesitate to shoot him."

"Don't worry, I warned him." Brad explained. "I'm sure that he's smiling because I'm out on a date with a beautiful woman."

"Thank you." She said, as she reached into her purse and retrieved the letter. "Shall we do it?"

Susan Fisher walked up behind her then, hearing this last question and clearing her throat.

"Hi." Brad said.

"Hi." She said. "I'm your waitress."

"Imagine that." Brad said. Susan Fisher giggled and Marcia looked at them sideways.

"Would you like something from the bar?"

"Sure." Brad said, looking to Marcia. "What would you like?"

"A glass of Chardonnay." Marcia answered.

Brad didn't know much about wine. He knew that there was proper wine etiquette, which involved looking at labels, sniffing corks and swishing it in the mouth. It all seemed very confusing, and he didn't want to embarrass himself. Still, he wasn't sure that a bottle of beer would be appropriate.

"Two glasses of Chardonnay." Brad told the waitress. He thought to himself that, if he remembered correctly this was a white wine. Would that mean that he would have to order fish? He seemed to remember that there were rules about that type of thing.

"Would you like the house chardonnay or would you like to see the wine list?" Susan Fisher asked.

Brad looked to Marcia, not sure what to say. He wouldn't know what to make of a wine list.

"The house Chardonnay is okay with me if it's okay with you." He told Marcia.

"It's fine." She said. "But you don't have to have wine if you usually drink something else."

"Oh no, I want to." Brad said, turning back to Susan. "Thanks. And could you do me a favor?…Could you tell Charlie to stop staring at us."

"Sure." She said, and went off to the bar.

"I want to get an idea of what life with you would be like." He told Marcia, explaining why he had ordered wine as well and trying to be romantic.

"Full of adventure." She said, handing him the envelope.

Bread and water was delivered to the table and Brad looked up at the busboy. He looked familiar.

"Hi. I'm Jim Hanson." He introduced himself. "You went to school with my sister Rita."

"Oh yeah..." Brad said. "...You're the kid who broke both legs on the slope your freshman year."

"Right." He smiled, and patted his legs. "All healed up now...Good as new."

"Great." Brad nodded as he went off. He looked over at Marcia. "It was this freak accident...He somehow got off in a sledding area and hit a toboggan that Father Murphy and a couple of sisters were on..."

Marcia looked down at the letter in his hands, bringing his attention back to it. He realized that she wanted to get right down to business. He held it in his hand and closed his eyes. The images came right away. He heard Susan Fisher come back to the table.

"Is he talking to the dead?" She asked Marcia.

"How did that rumor get started, anyway?..." Brad asked, opening his eyes.

"I heard it from a girl who works at a store where your Aunt Jane shops." She explained.

"Did she mention that my Aunt Jane is mentally ill?"

"Well, everyone knows that..." She said in a very matter of fact manner, before returning to her role. "Have you looked at your menus yet?"

"What are the specials tonight?" Marcia asked. Brad knew that she wanted to order, so that they could get back to the letter without further interruptions.

"They're paper clipped right inside the menu." Susan explained. "The salmon in a garlic cheese sauce is supposed to be very good."

"I'll have to look at the menu a bit." Marcia said, seeming a bit underwhelmed.

"Okay." Susan turned to Brad and smiled. "I was just kidding about you talking to the dead, Brad…"

He nodded, and she walked away. He looked at Marcia and found her looking at him.

"How long have you had the gift?" She asked.

"I think that I got it when I was thirteen, although it took awhile for me notice that I had it."

"It just started one day?"

"Well, it all started with a foreign exchange student named Pia…"

Jim Hanson walked up then and filled their water glasses.

"I heard about her…my older brother Tommy was one of the guys…" He started.

"Listen Jim, we're talking here…" Marcia said, being a bit curt.

"Sorry." Jim Hanson shrugged and exited. It was apparent that she wasn't at all accustom to small town life.

"My older brother Thomas hosted a foreign exchange student. In retrospect, it seems odd that they would send a blond, blued eyed, Swedish girl to stay with a male high school student in a small Midwestern town…it was probably some sort of experiment."

"No doubt."

"It's my understanding that after the controversy and all, they changed the rules, so that it would never happen again."

"What's supposed to be good here?" Marcia asked. He knew that she was anxious to find out what he could learn from the letter. Yet, she was being a very good sport, chatting with him about his gift and looking at the menu.

"The fish." Brad told her.

"What kind is caught out there and prepared fresh?"

"I'm not sure...I'm not much of a fisherman. Trout I think."
Susan Fisher walked up.

"Ready to order?"

"What's fresh?"

"Lake trout...caught fresh today and sauteed in butter and cream sauce. And perch, caught up at Willit's lake, also delivered today...it's done in a beer batter and served with French fries."

"Could I get something prepared without butter, cream, batter or oil?"

"You're not from around here are you?" Susan looked down at Marcia. As Marcia looked up at her, Brad imagined that she would be quite curt, but rather she smiled and seemed very polite.

"Actually I am...I just moved away for awhile."

"Oh...You didn't go to school in Bay Springs though..." It was Susan's attempt to bring Brad and herself back into that world where they were all kids from the same high school.

"No, I didn't."

Well, I'll tell you honey...you certainly don't need to be on a diet..."

Brad had never really understood women and was never sure when they were being catty or when it was just casual conversation. He had sensed that these two didn't really like each other for what ever reason, but he wasn't sure of any of it.

"I know that." Marcia told Susan.

"Oh."

"I'm not on a diet...I just try to eat healthy..."

"Ah, what the hell?...we're all going to die." It seemed to Brad that Susan might be feeling a little depressed.

"What are you going to have?" Marcia turned to Brad.

"No, no...you first." He said, trying to be a gentleman.

"Let's see..." Marcia studied the menu. "Do you have a pasta dish?

"Yes, fettucine alfredo."

"Do you have a salad bar?"

"Yes, of course."

"I'd like the salad bar."

"Just the salad bar?"

"Yes."

"No meat?"

"No."

"How about you Brad?" Susan turned to him and smiled very sweetly.

"I'd like the fettucine alfredo."

"With the salad bar?"

"Yes. Actually, I don't really like salad, so she can have my salad bar..."

"That would be sharing...You're not allowed to do that." She told him.

"Is that like a law?" He asked, understanding that this was not proper restaurant etiquette, but taking issue with it all a bit.

"Yes."

"A Federal law or a restaurant law?"

"Okay, I'll do it..." Susan said, finally. "But Harry doesn't like it."

"Who's Harry?" Marcia asked.

"He's the owner." Susan answered, writing on the order pad and not looking at Marcia.

"And he's like your Uncle or something, right?" Brad asked

"Yes...My mother's older brother."

Susan took the menus, smiled at him again and walked away.

"Wow, it's like everyone is related to each other in this town." Marcia said.

"Sometimes it seems like that..." He nodded.

"I sure hope that we're not related."

"Me too." Brad smiled and thought to himself that she was flirting with him a bit.

"So having this Swedish foreign exchange student caused you to have this gift…"

"Well, indirectly. You see she was very…well…for my little brother and I, she provided our first glimpse of the, um, glory of womanhood. I think that my mother thought we were glimpsing too much, so she planned a summer trip. My older brother was allowed to stay home with Pia, which was a big mistake, while Mom, Dad, my little brother and I traveled through the Civil War battlegrounds, the Appalachian mountains and into the deep South…"

"This was when you were thirteen?…"

"Right. We stayed in a small town near New Orleans one night and we attended this party the locals were having. There was this sort of ceremony being performed there. All I remember was drumming, a chicken and this woman dancing around half dressed. My father was enjoying it and drinking beer. My mother was terribly shocked by this ceremony and she rushed my little brother and I out. It was very strange, at least very different than the parties we have here."

"Or in New York."

"Really?"

"Well, I probably hung out with a more conservative crowd."

"Anyway, my father stayed, and we didn't see him again until the next afternoon. He wouldn't tell my mother what had happened, and they argued about it for years afterward…"

"Wow."

"It was really when all of their problems started."

Susan Fisher walked up to the table then.

"The plates are up at the salad bar if you want to go ahead and serve yourself." She told Marcia.

"Thanks."

"Why don't you go ahead." Brad told her. "Charlie is still over there looking at us...I'll go over and have a word with him."

"Okay."

Marcia got up and headed to the salad bar, while Brad walked over to the bar. Charlie was just standing there, staring at him, apparently a bit intoxicated.

"Hey, Charlie..."

"Hey, cousin..." He gave Brad a big, stupid smile.

"What are you doing staring at us?"

"Oh, I'm sorry, I didn't notice that I was..."

"Well, you are...And we're trying to have a sort of a romantic dinner over there..."

"Oh, okay, cool...I'll stay out of the way...Listen, do you think that maybe you can put in a good word for me, to try to help me with Cyndi and all..."

Marcia was picking through the salad bar items, selectively placing vegetables on her plate. As Brad walked toward the salad bar, Mary, from the apparel store, walked up behind her. He stopped near their table, close enough to hear their conversation.

"Hi." Mary said.

Marcia turned, surprised to see her there.

"Oh, hi..."

"I'm so embarrassed...I didn't know that you were dating Brad when you came in the store...I wouldn't have said those things..."

"Actually, this is our first date..." Marcia continued to place choice vegetables on her plate. "We haven't really known each other for very long."

"You mean that you decided to go out with him, knowing that I liked him?"

Mary seemed shocked, then squinted and pursed her lips.

"Well, yes, but..." Marcia stuttered and stepped back.

Brad decided to walk up then. Seeing him, Mary turned and smiled sweetly.

"Hi Brad."

"Hi Mary." He nodded, a little uncomfortable, but feeling he should rescue Marcia.

"Are you here having dinner with a date?" Marcia asked Mary, having gained her composure and glancing around the room.

"Oh...no, I'm just having a drink with my girlfriends." She said. Her tone became different, a bit sing-song when she turned and addressed Brad. "Your cousin Charlie bought us all drinks."

"Yes, he's something..." Brad nodded. Marcia moved closer to him and looked at Mary with raised eyebrows. It was a subtle, but apparent act of victory and possession. Mary took it in and Brad was flattered by the whole thing.

"Well, I'll leave you two alone." Mary said, turning and making her exit. Marcia and Brad returned to their table, and didn't say anything to each other for a moment. To avoid a conversation about Mary, Brad started talking.

"When we got back from our summer trip, we found that the entire football team, junior and varsity, had been thrown in jail. Pia was at the house and she was very happy to see us, explaining that it was all her fault and that we had to do something. My father went to see the Sheriff, who tried to convince him to file charges of statutory rape against the dozens of students who were locked up in the cell. The Sheriff claimed that it was his duty as a "foreign exchange father" to see that the right thing was done. Pia went along with him, to explain that she hadn't been forced to do anything and that they were all very nice boys. My father didn't know what to do, but filing charges meant that all of them, including his eldest son, would stay in jail and have a criminal record. He decided to have nothing to do with it and they were all released. Pia's visit to the United States was cut short. A large percentage of young men in this town lost their innocence that summer and I received the gift."

"Wow, that's quite a story."

"Yes, I know."

"I still don't understand how you got your gift."

"Either do I, but it happened that summer and all of that had something to do with it."

They drank their wine for a moment, smiling at each other and not saying anything.

"Can you ask my grandparents a question for me?"

"Sure."

"Can you ask them if the story about my uncle being a gangster is true?"

"Wow, a gangster, eh?"

"That's what I've heard."

"Okay."

Brad held the letter, and closed his eyes. This time, his eyes remained closed for a very long time. He heard Tim the busboy come over and fill their water glasses. He sensed that he was looking at him and that Marcia motioned for him to exit without saying anything.

Brad opened his eyes to see Marcia looking toward the bar. Mary was there, having a drink with a couple of girlfriends. They were all looking at Brad and Marcia and talking. Charlie was trying not to watch them. Marcia glanced back at Brad and found him watching her.

"Your Uncle Claude was married to a woman called Babe, who he met in Chicago." He explained. "He had left here as a child…He was a juvenile delinquent, and was sent away to a special school. Sort of like you, eh?"

"Sort of."

"In the nineteen-twenties, your grandparents were newly-weds and ran for a time with a fast crowd. Claude was the fastest of them all and he came to head up a gang of criminals. They were organized, well armed and ambitious. Within a short period of time they were being sought by the FBI for a chain of bank robberies in the Midwest."

"Wow."

"Your grandparents had settled down and bought a small farm in the North Woods. They came to be God fearing, hard working people. After a long run of luck and years on the run, Claude and his gang returned here as well, thinking that they could buy farm land and retire. Federal Agents were one step ahead of them, waiting in the cornfields on the family property. You know, it's the same property you live on now...the same cornfield where I met you.

"I've heard the stories of the bank robberies...And that my uncle was killed in a gunfight with the FBI."

Brad picked the letter back up, and closed his eyes again. After a moment, he continued.

"A half dozen federal agents were in the cornfield, armed with sophisticated weaponry. As Uncle Claude and his gang pulled into the drive, the Federal Agents started shooting. Having their weapons close at hand, the gang found cover and started firing back. Uncle Claude made it into the cabin where your grandparents lived. They were on the floor, having been interrupted in the middle of dinner by the gunfire.

"Sorry about all this, brother." Claude said, making his way over to the window and firing into the cornfield.

It was a full scale battle, lasting for over an hour. The wounded fell in the dirt, continuing to shoot until their final breath. Slowly the gunfire let up and it was over.

"I think we got them." Uncle Claude said, turning around to reveal that he had been shot twice in the chest. He fell to the floor and his brother quickly went to his aid. Claude looked up at him and whispered his final words. "My bags are in the trunk...can you bring them in?"

Claude closed his eyes and died, a peaceful look upon his face.

"What happened next?"

"Once the gunfire had stopped, your grandparents crawled over and opened the door. The entire gang lay in the drive, covered in blood. No sound came from the cornfield. They called out, but no one answered. Eventually they ventured out to explore and surmise the situation. All of the Federal Agents lay in the cornfield, shot down in the line of duty.

After checking to see if anyone needed medical aid and finding that no one was alive, they returned to the cabin.

"What should we do?" Your grandma asked.

"Get Claude's bags out of the trunk." Your grandpa answered, getting up and going back outside.

When he returned he had an odd look on his face and two suitcases full of cash.

"What should we do?" Your grandma asked.

Brad closed his eyes again for a moment, holding the letter tight. He wanted to be certain that he understood. What they did was quite a surprise. He handed the letter back to Marcia. She had finished most of her wine.

"Would you like another glass?" Brad asked.

"No." She said. "Tell me...what do you know?"

"Do you think we'll ever go out together again...After I've answered all of your questions?"

Marcia looked him straight in the eye and spoke firmly.

"If you help me find the money, I'll give you a percentage."

Brad nodded. He didn't care about money this evening, he cared about her. Yet, it was apparent how important it was to her. She wasn't in a romantic mood at all and she was anxious to get down to business. He sighed and told her the remainder of the story.

"Your grandmother and grandfather were of a character distinctly different than your Uncle Claude. While he felt that rules were meant to be broken and that you made your own luck in this life, they were fairly puritanical. They felt that it would be wrong to spend the money. Yet, they didn't want to contact the authorities and bring shame to the family name. So they decided to do a rather odd thing."

"What's that?"

"Now, mind you, your family homestead was even more remote in those days, then it is now. No one had seen the shoot out, and it was likely that no one had heard it, or would come to investigate. So, they took the bodies of the dead Feds and the members of the gang and buried them in the cornfield."

"And the money?"

"They buried it as well."

"Wow."

"And everyone thinks that I have an odd family…Isn't it sort of scary, knowing that you have all those people buried out in your cornfield?"

"Well, I didn't know about it before now. I suppose I'll find out if it bothers me tonight when I go home to bed."

Brad considered saying something suggestive about the end of the evening and going to bed, then tried to decide how to say it in a romantic fashion. Susan arrived with the food then and the moment passed.

"More wine?" Susan asked.

He noticed that Marcia had almost finished hers, while he had hardly touched his. He drank it down steadily, then set down the glass.

"More wine?" He asked Marcia.

"Yes, please."

"Yes, please." Brad said to Susan, who smiled and went off. He looked at his pasta and tasted it. Marcia nibbled on a carrot.

"And they wanted me to tell you, that the decision is yours whether or not to act on this information."

"How so?"

"They didn't say more than that."

"Well, they decided not to touch the money and to leave the truth buried there for the rest of their lives..." Marcia said, after a moment.

"Indeed."

"So they're probably suggesting that I do the same...Maybe trying to warn me from the other side."

"Actually, I don't think that they're allowed to warn you from the other side. It seems like there's a rule against it or something. They aren't making any suggestion at all. The way they put it wasn't, don't do it or, you shouldn't do it. They said that the decision was yours."

"Could you ask them what they mean, exactly?"

"That's all they wanted to say."

"Weird." Marcia shook her head and looked away.

Brad noticed that Mary was talking to Susan, as she waited for their wine at the bar. He looked away, not wanting Marcia to notice.

"Are you talking about what they said, or the fact that I can communicate with the dead? He asked.

"Oh, your gift is really cool, that's not a problem at all...It's just weird that, well, you figure that if the dead could talk they could tell you so much…And it turns out that they are just as hard to understand as the living."

"It's true." Brad laughed and shook his head in agreement. It was one of the first things he had realized when he began to use the gift. "It sure is different than in the movies, isn't it?"

Susan returned with their wine.

"You're not trying to get your date drunk are you, Brad?" She said, putting the glasses in front of them.

"I don't know…Is wine good for that sort of thing?"

"It works on me." Susan offered.

"I'll bet." Marcia agreed.

Susan was a bit taken back and made her exit.

"I apologize…I shouldn't have brought you here." Brad said.

"Oh, no…I like it here."

"But, all of the interruptions."

"It's just small town life." Marcia shrugged. "I'll have to get accustom to it."

"Oh?…Are you planning on staying?"

"I don't know. Life in the city can be difficult and life here is so different. I'm on a leave of absence from work…part of me wants to quit, but part of me likes what I do."

"Is it a good job?"

"It pays well and it's a position that a lot of people want. But I don't really like my boss and what I would really like is to be independent…"

"…And you have a boyfriend back there…" Brad added.

"Yes, sort of…how did you know?"

"Had a feeling…But you're thinking about dumping him, aren't you?" He asked, hopefully.

"Yes."

"Is he a jerk?"

"Yes, sort of…" She looked serious for a moment, then smiled.

"Not at all like me, I'm sure."

"That's for sure."

"And I take it that's good…"

Marcia smiled and nodded her head.

Marcia created a plan over dinner. The way she had it figured was that to keep it all secret, the two of them would have to do all of the digging in the dark. She explained that it wouldn't be right that Brad get an equal share; after all it was her family's money. She felt that ten percent would be fair.

"You do realize that what you're talking about involves digging up dead bodies, right?" He couldn't believe that she actually wanted to do it.

"Twenty percent." She shot back.

Having already given him a bigger cut, she then sensed that the real problem was not the money but the idea of the bodies.

"Look…I doubt that Grandma and Grandpa took the time to build coffins, right?…If they've been buried in the dirt, they've probably decayed to the point that they're just skeletons."

"Gosh, you make it sound so much more pleasant than I envisioned it." Brad explained. "Actually, if it's family money, I probably shouldn't have anything to do with it at all…maybe you and your sister and your dad should dig it all up."

"Oh, but I don't want for my dad to know…"

"Why?"

"He won't share the money. He'll say that he's the rightful heir and that it belongs to him. He'll explain that it will be passed on to us, but go right ahead and spend all of it."

"I see." Brad said.

"Actually, it could be pleasant…" Marcia smiled at him, as if to suggest something beyond a larger percentage. "I have to admit that I'm actually looking forward to spending the night with you out in the cornfield…"

"…With the rotting corpses." He added, looking unenthusiastic, but thinking that perhaps it might have an upside.

Brad and Marcia talked very little on the way home. She didn't seem to notice and was smiling at him most of the time. When he pulled in the driveway, he wasn't certain that he should kiss her. Yet, he had the opportunity and did. And she kissed him…in a more intense manner and much beyond what he had expected. Driving home, Brad was very happy.

After the Date

"How was your date?" Cyndi asked her as she came through the door.

Marcia looked at her little sister, stretched out on the sofa in front of the television, with a bag of potato chips on her lap and a beer in her hand.

"Fine."

"And Brad?..."

"And Brad what?..."

"How is he?"

"He's nice...you know, he's not really like I thought he was that first day...not really like Charlie at all."

"Charlie's nice..." Cyndi sat up a bit, ready to defend him. "I don't know why you don't like him..."

"I'm sorry Cyndi." Having spent so many years away from her little sister, she was happy to spend time with her and didn't want to argue with her or upset her. "It's just that I think you could do better."

"For one, a lot of girls want Charlie. He's considered quite a catch. And besides..." Cyndi shrank back down in the sofa, her breath catching in her throat and her eyes filling with water.

"Oh, Cyn..." Marcia went over and knelt at her side. "What is it?"

"I love him." She said.

"Oh…" Marcia smiled. "I was worried that you were going to say you were pregnant."

"No, but…" Cyndi's words came hard and she tried to breath slowly. "You weren't around all these years…You don't know how it is…"

"Tell me…"

"When I was in school, the kids made fun of me…they called me space case…And I'm sure that they still do. That's why I don't go into Bay Springs very often…"

"But Cyndi…you're a beautiful girl…and you're brain is just the same as everybody else's…"

"Is not…"

"Sure it is, you just think to much about other things…like matters of the heart. You're sensitive…that's better than being intellectual."

"What's intellectual?"

The phone rang then and Cyndi jumped up to get it.

"Oh…I'll bet Charlie is calling me…"

Marcia considered for a moment what an odd world she had fallen into. She had always believed herself to be highly intelligent, and to have excellent coping mechanisms. Living in New York City, she had to be prepared for a number of situations, from shrewd lawyers to armed assailants. However, this was something else all together; this small Northern town. It was a place where everyone seemed aware of and even intimate with each other. She sensed that might have been the case with Brad and their waitress. And everyone in the bar seemed to be watching the whole thing as though it were theater, or a favorite situation comedy.

Marcia turned her attention to the television. A news program was on and they were talking about a controversy and a freak accident. A New York art collector of some note and the receptionist at a top gallery had been killed. Details were still sketchy, but apparently they had been making love beneath a grand piano, which had collapsed, and fallen to the floor, crushing them. Hanging over the piano was a painting by a primitive artist named Jimmy Snakespirit. This was of note because over a dozen people had met their fates over the last few months, in homes where the artist's work was hung.

"Wow." Marcia said to herself. "There's a book waiting to be written there."

She found herself thinking about work and the publishing world, but tried not to. She was on vacation, perhaps permanently. It wasn't publishing that she hated...in fact she had always loved books and the stories behind them. She suspected that one day, when she married, it would be to an author. What she really wanted, and dreamed of, was having her own small publishing house. Something that she could run herself, creating special, highly personal works for the large audience she believed to be out there. Perhaps if they were actually able to find the buried money, she could make it all happen. It would certainly enable her to help Cyndi, who seemed to believe that her only hope was in marrying a white trash local.

Marcia looked over at Cyndi, who was twirling her hair with her finger as she smiled and talked on the phone. Her sadness was gone now, and she seemed truly happy. Was Charlie really so bad? The only thing which set him apart from the dozens of men she had met in New York was his simple, redneck approach to life. If he was actually to get a divorce, and if he could take care of Cyndi, perhaps they would be happy together.

Marcia knew that she couldn't expect Cyndi to want the same things in life, or be at all like her. In fact, Marcia knew that it was difficult enough to live up to her own high standards. Taking a break from her life with a man she quite possibly hated, she too was finding herself attracted to a local. She wondered to herself if she could learn to be happy living in the North Woods. If she could be an ordinary girl.

When Brad arrived home, Sarah Mitchell was pacing and terribly upset. Aunt Jane was sitting on the sofa, shaking her head. A home shopping program was on, but they weren't looking at the television screen. Brad knew that it had to be very serious, as Aunt Jane rarely missed an opportunity to shop from television. His mother was usually right by her side, making sure that she was only taking advantage of the bargains.

"It's terrible!" Mother shouted, running toward him.

"What?" Brad asked, as she held him tight, trembling.

"It's your Father…he's been kidnapped."

"What?" Brad was so shocked that he pushed his mother away, searching her face for a suggestion of sanity. "Why would anyone kidnap him?"

"I know who it is…and I know where he is…" Sarah Mitchell explained. She walked slowly over to the sofa and stood near Aunt Jane. "It's those voodoo people in Louisiana…They have him."

"What voodoo people?" He asked. She shrugged at first and walked the other direction. It seemed to him like denial and he felt that it was a subject which needed to be addressed.

"We first met them on our summer vacation…" She started. "Remember that time we went to Gettysburg, and drove down through the Appalachian mountains into the South?"

"Sure." Brad said, Dad still takes that route often on sales calls.

"Yes, well, he went back to see those people…I don't know why…"

"Your mother thinks that the people are evil." Aunt Jane added.

"Well, I think that the fact they kidnapped my husband is proof of that." She snapped at her.

Aunt Jane looked shocked and saddened, as Sarah Mitchell was rarely snappy. Looking at her sister, a look of shame and love came across her face.

"I'm sorry Jane." She said. "I'm under a lot of stress. I think that I'll make some muffins…that will cheer up this situation."

She started toward the kitchen.

"Wait Mother." Brad said. "Are you saying that Dad has been kidnapped by some sort of voodoo people?"

Mother stopped and turned. She hesitated a moment, sighing a bit, then motioned for him to follow her into the kitchen.

"They want for you to go down there." She explained as she gathered the ingredients for muffins. "They say that they don't want to harm either of you, but that they just need for you to help them with a ceremony."

It certainly sounded like a major problem. It appeared that Brad would have to go on the trip to help his kidnapped father. All of this couldn't have come along at a worse possible time, what with Marcia depending on him. But then, this business of digging into a mass grave in the middle of the night sounded like it could be a problem as well.

Sarah Mitchell went on to tell Brad what she knew of the story. It was all new to him, as he'd never really known how he came to have the gift. Later he would hear his fathers side and then Jimmy Snakespirit's story. At this point he found it all a bit of a shock. He decided to call Marcia and tell her the story, to find out what she thought.

He found that Charlie was using the telephone.

"I'm talking to Cyndi." Charlie explained.

"Ask if I can talk to Marcia for a moment…" Brad asked, using his best "we're buddies because we're cousins" voice.

"Yeah, just a second." Charlie said. "Listen baby…Brad wants to know if he can talk to your sister…okay, thanks…"

He reached out to hand Brad the receiver.

"She went to get her. I want Cyndi back when you're done."

Brad nodded, took the phone and waited for Marcia to come on the line.

"How sweet of you to phone…" She said. "I had a wonderful time tonight…"

"Listen…" He started. "I might need to put off helping you with your midnight digging project."

"Well, thanks a lot." She said, hanging up the phone.

Brad wandered out of the room, not certain what his next step should be.

"Is Cyndi on the line?…" Charlie was standing in the hallway.

"No…Marcia hung up on me."

"So call her back." It was the first time his cousin Charlie had ever made sense to him.

"Yeah, okay…" Brad said, going back in and dialing the phone. Marcia answered.

"Hello, Marcia…"

"So let's hear the story." She said.

"It's a long one."

"I'll listen."

"Okay." He said. He sat down and started to explain.

Charlie popped back into the room then.

"Can I talk to Cyndi?"

"Uh, actually I'm still talking to Marcia."

"I thought that she hung up on you."

"Yes but now she's letting me explain."

"Hey, love means never having to say you're sorry."

"Listen Charlie…Just give me another minute."

Brad asked Marcia to come and see him in the morning, to give him a chance to explain it all.

Considering Her

"You really believe it?" Randy had asked one day, when he and Brad were hanging out in the field of abandoned cars.

"Believe what?" Brad asked. He was sitting in an old Buick. Randy was sitting on the roof of a nearby Cadillac, strumming his guitar.

"That she's out there…" He was referring to the lyrics that he was putting chords to; one of Brad's poems that he could easily turn into a song.

"Sure." Brad said.

"And that she'll come to you?"

"Sure…" Brad had always believed in destiny. His life seemed so odd, and the only explanation was that there was some purpose to it all.

"Yeah, but why should she come to you? Destiny is something that you've got to go out and grab. Success as a writer…the woman of your dreams…you think that you can just hang out in these woods and it will come to you."

Brad didn't answer and Randy stopped waiting for him to. He started to strum his guitar again and to sing Brad's words:

"I know, one day…She'll walk through my door…and so I stay…

So alone, waiting at home.

When I go out, I'm not just lookin'…
I know when we meet, I'll be totally took in."

Meeting Marcia brought that talk back to Brad, a memory he didn't realize he had. Brad didn't usually remember much about his past, just the way he felt about the people and the times. Perhaps it was because of the gift. His mind was so full of the lives of others, that there was little room for his own past. Occasionally, Brad would remember something from when he was a child; when his mother and father loved each other and they all seemed so much like an ordinary family.

What Brad wanted to remember was that trip down South and the events at the Voodoo ceremony which had started this chain of events.

As Marcia and Brad walked together, down the road from his home, he told her what he knew.

"And that's it…" He added finally, awaiting her response.

"Wow."

"Yes, indeed…"

"You just had to out do my story didn't you?…" Marcia smiled and rolled her eyes.

"Believe me, that was the last thing I wanted to do…"

"Is that Mr. Ellison?" Marcia asked. Brad turned to see that the old man was walking up the road toward them.

"Yeah…He goes for a walk everyday. He's probably healthier than I am."

They watched as Mr. Ellison approached them, taking long strides and swinging his arms. Once he got close, they noticed that he was sweating and gasping for air.

"Good morning young lady…" He said. "Good morning Brad."

"Good morning." Marcia said.

"Hi." Brad nodded. He was worried that someone Mr. Ellison's age shouldn't be getting so much exercise.

"You two sure make a smart looking couple."

"Thanks." Marcia smiled and looked at Brad. He appreciated Mr. Ellison saying it, but hoped that he might continue on without saying too much, as was the habit of his mother and Aunt Jane.

"Well, I won't keep you two...I can see that you're having a very important talk."

"See you." Brad said, as Mr. Ellison continued down the road.

As he watched him walk away, Brad told himself that Mr. Ellison was probably in excellent shape for his age and that he shouldn't be concerned. They walked a while, then Brad turned and looked back at Mr. Ellison, who turned around as well, and waved.

"He seems like a really sweet guy." Marcia said.

"Yeah, he is." They stopped by the side of the road to rest and watch a group of horses in a field. Brad leaned on the wood fence and Marcia settled close to him.

"How old is Mr. Ellison?"

"I'm not sure."

They watched walk into the distance. Marcia turned and looked at Brad.

"It's strange that the two of you are close. I mean, the difference in your ages and all..."

"Yeah. It all started because of the gift, you know..." He started to explain, then hesitated. She was listening intently and he felt he should go on and tell her. "I would hang out at the Historical Society, because it was so interesting communicating with all of the people who lived here so long ago...And I was able to put him in touch with old friends and I got to know him...and his world."

"I got the feeling that he had a thing for my Great Aunt Christine."

"Yeah, he loved her. And still loves her, I guess…He still pines for her."

"What does that saying mean?…" Marcia stopped him, perhaps to lighten things up. "Pines for her…"

"I don't know, really…Up here in the woods we have sayings like that, and they seem perfectly natural, although it's hard to figure out how they started. Maybe it has something to do with pine trees…gosh, I'd hate to think it, but maybe it has to do with pine coffins…"

"So, why is it that he never asked you to contact her? He told me that she moved off to the city and he never heard from her. Most people don't live so long, so you probably could have found out…"

"I did."

"You did?"

"Yes. He found her signature in an old album the other day…As it turns out, she fell on hard times in the city, and died at a young age. She didn't have any memory of Mr. Ellison. He fell in love, but apparently failed to make any impression on her…"

Neither of them said anything for a moment. He noticed that Marcia's eyes had filled with water. They started to walk back toward the house.

"I'm sorry…I shouldn't have told you. I wasn't thinking, I mean, she was your Aunt…"

"No it's not that…" Marcia shook her head and dried her eyes on the sleeve of her shirt. "It must have broke his heart…"

"Well, it broke mine, so I decided not to tell him. He's an old man and I don't know what sort of condition his heart is in. I thought that it would be irresponsible to break it…"

"I can understand that…So, listen, what are you going to do about saving your father from these Voodoo people?"

"Well, I guess that I have to go down there." Brad said it as if he was convinced that it was the thing to do and that he could do it.

"I'll go with you."

"What?"

"Maybe I can help you out…"

"Oh sure, then I'll be indebted to you and have to help you dig up the money and dead bodies."

"We're not going to dig up the dead bodies…Only the money." Marcia wasn't looking at him, as though she couldn't. "Besides, that's not why I want to go with you."

"So why do you want to go?"

"None of your business…" Marcia looked at him now, right in the eye, seeming very defiant. She smiled and looked away again.

"You know that it could be dangerous…I mean voodoo kidnappers don't sound like nice people." Brad explained as he thought to himself that, yes, it would be nice to spend the time with her.

"Maybe that's it…That I want to make sure that you get back safely."

"Maybe you care about me." He offered.

Marcia smiled and they arrived back at the driveway. Brad was now convinced that he should have a talk with Marcia's Aunt Christine. He knew that Mr. Ellison's walk would take him a distance from the Historical Society and he knew where an extra key was kept hidden outside the building. Brad and Marcia climbed into his car and headed out.

Brad found the book in the top drawer of his desk; the page with the signature marked with a fresh rose petal. A moment later, Christine Roberts was standing there, smiling and apparently happy to see him again.

"Oh, hello." She said. "I was thinking about your Mr. Ellison. That must be Leonard Ellison...and I do remember him. His family lived on Main Street and I would often see him on my way to work at the Hotel. We danced one night at a church social. He was a very sweet man. He was very shy though and didn't say much. I guess I made a lasting impression on him..."

"Well, he never forgot that dance." Brad told her. "In fact, he fell in love with you."

"In love with me?"

"Yes. He still thinks about you all the time. He imagines that if you'd stayed in town, he might have married you."

"I had no idea. But, yes, I guess it's possible. I wish that I'd never left, of course, and imagine that we could have had a happy life together. I guess it just wasn't in the cards."

"Well, you may meet again."

"Yes." She answered. "I hope we do."

Marcia and Brad put the book where they'd found it, locked up and left. Driving back up the road, they passed Mr. Ellison. He smiled and waved, having no idea what they were up to. Brad felt a little guilty, pulling the wool over the eyes of a man he had a great deal of respect for. At the same time, he felt really good about the whole thing.

A Road Trip

Brad was convinced that he had to go after his father, although he was not convinced that he was up to it. Marcia had insisted that he take her along. Brad figured that would mean at least a couple of nights in motel rooms with her and that the situation wasn't all bad. They agreed to leave early in the morning.

"You're so brave." Sarah Mitchell said, holding Brad as though he were going off to war and stroking his hair.

"I'll be okay, Mother." He said pulling himself away.

"Be careful!" Aunt Jane shouted, as he headed down the driveway.

"Don't worry." Brad waved and got into his car. As he started it up and pulled away, he waved at Mother and Aunt Jane. He couldn't help but consider that his life had been so routine a few days before. Now he was going off to rescue his father from Voodoo people, after which he planned to help the girl that he was falling in love with dig up dead people and buried treasure.

When Brad pulled up in front of Marcia's place, he found her standing out by the side of the road with a suitcase. She wasn't wearing any makeup and she wore baggy pants and a sweatshirt. He thought to himself that she looked pretty good. He considered that even on an off day, or early in the morning, she would be able to talk him into just about anything.

"We'll start digging as soon as we get back." Brad told her, as she climbed into the car.

She smiled, reaching over and kissing him on the cheek.

They drove into town, stopping by Tim's house. Marcia waited in the car, as Brad went up and rang the bell. Tim's mother came to the door, and went to get him.

"Oh, hi Brad." Tim said, walking up in red pajamas.

Brad reached out and handed him the keys to the pizza parlor.

"I need for you to care for the restaurant for a few days..." Brad explained, as Tim looked at the keys and his mouth hung open. "I have to leave town for a bit."

"But, I've only worked a few days...I don't think I'm ready..."

"I trust you." Brad said.

"What about the owners?"

"I don't want to bother them with this." Brad turned and walked away. "You'll be fine."

He didn't look back, because he knew that Tim would be standing there in his red pajamas, with his mouth hanging open. There was a good chance that he wouldn't be able to deal with it, and that Brad would lose his job. Yet, he felt that he was doing what he had to do. And he was making the trip with a girl who was very attractive. Strangely, Brad wasn't really nervous...he felt really good.

The North Woods were far removed from everything else. It took half the day just to get out of the state. Brad and Marcia talked about art and theater. She had a great interest in both and he knew nothing about either.

"I once read that many abstract expressionists believed that forgetting how to paint was the first step toward painting." Marcia would say.

"Oh." Brad would say.

Once they got on the subject of books, they were fine. He read a great deal and they enjoyed many of the same authors. Conversation usually returned to each other, a subject they were equally unfamiliar with.

"A week ago, I didn't even know you existed." Brad told her, as she laid down in the front seat, her head resting near his thigh.

"It is strange isn't it."

"Well, we're getting to know each other anyway…"

"When we get back, maybe I can get to know your family better and meet your friends."

"I don't have any really…I mean you've met Mr. Ellison, and my best friend Randy, he's…"

"I know." She glanced up at him, then went back to looking up and out the window. "Your mom told me…That must have been tough."

"Still is." Brad said. Neither of them said anything for a moment and he thought it best to change the subject. "I work a lot, and sometimes go out for a drink with guys from town. And I spend time with my family and Charlie…and his wife Tina. Sometimes Tina and I go to the movies together."

"Aha, so you've got a thing going with Charlie's wife…"

She sounded a little jealous and he decided to leave it at that. It was better than having her know that he'd long been without a girlfriend. With no close friends or lovers, Brad suspected that he seemed every bit as odd as the rest of his family.

They drove deep into the night. Brad knew that he probably could have driven further. He was, of course, in a hurry to rescue his father. Yet, he and Marcia were getting along very well and he was anxious to spend that first night in a motel room.

"God..." Marcia said, as they pulled into a motel parking lot. "I'm not used to driving all day...Do you think we're half way there?"

"Almost." He got out of the car, his legs aching. They walked to the motel office and went inside. There was no one there, but the bell on the door rang and they could hear a television in the next room. An old man walked out and looked them over as he walked up to the counter.

"Good timing." He said. "It's a commercial."

"What's on?" Marcia asked, being friendly.

"It's Thursday night." He said, in a very matter of fact manner. "There's only one show to watch on Thursday night."

Marcia and Brad looked at each other and shrugged their shoulders when he wasn't looking.

"How many nights?"

"Just one." Brad told him.

"Just passing through, eh?"

"Yep."

"Not often we have out of towners...Usually they drive on into the city."

"We were tired."

Brad looked up to see a sign above the desk, offering complimentary adult films. Having been brought up in a town full of very religious people and having rarely left it, he was taken a bit by surprise. He saw Marcia look up at the sign. He wasn't sure what she was thinking, but thought that he should be every bit the gentleman.

"We, um, don't need the movies." Brad said.

"They come with the room." The old man explained. "They're already hooked up. Your name?..."

"Brad Mitchell."

"Major credit card?..."

He'd never really had a need for a credit card, so he had never gotten one.

"I'll be paying cash." Brad said.

"That's fine, but I'll still need a credit card number." The old man said, he looked at the clock, concerned that he might miss part of his television program.

"Why?" Brad asked.

"Motel policy."

"I don't have a credit card." Brad admitted. He was a bit embarrassed in front of Marcia.

"I do." She said. She took a credit card out of her purse, and handed it to the old man.

"Car license number?..." He inquired.

"I don't know my car license number." Brad said, shrugging his shoulders.

"So, go outside and see what it is..." The old man seemed terribly inconvenienced. Brad wanted to finish this business and get the key to their room. He walked outside and across the parking lot.

Brad read the number and, repeating it over and over to himself, went back in the office.

"Thank you." The old man was saying to Marcia, handing her the key. "It's the fifth door down on the right. There's one of those personal coffee makers and packets of coffee in the room. Before you use it, you'd better rinse it out though...We sometimes have this problem with bugs."

Perhaps he realized that Marcia and Brad weren't thrilled to hear this.

"But not with bed bugs." He added.

"Thanks." Marcia said and they headed out to their room.

"I saw a coffee shop across the street." Brad told Marcia. "We'll go there in the morning."

"Okay." She said. When they arrived at the room, she unlocked the door and turned on the light.

They stood there, staring at the double bed for a moment and he again thought it would be best to act as a gentleman. After all, she might have objected to the situation and he wanted to be sensitive to that.

"Oh, I'll go down and tell him that we should have separate beds." Brad offered, not moving in that direction with great haste.

"He says this is all he has." Marcia explained.

"Oh." He said. "Then, I'll go and get the bags."

He had been prepared for the worst; that Marcia would not want to sleep with him, or that she would laugh when she saw him naked. What he experienced was the greatest night of his life. They were nasty and they were romantic. He went from passion to exhaustion and back again all night long. He went so far as to propose to her at one point. This she laughed off, covering his mouth with hers. Brad couldn't help thinking that he wanted a lot of this for a long time to come.

"You're right…" Marcia said, as she fell asleep in his arms. "…We don't need the movies."

In the morning, they were still friends. They had breakfast and talked about past relationships.

"Have you ever been in love?" She asked. He looked at her and didn't answer. He didn't know what to say. "You know, like when you've spent years with someone…"

"Oh, that kind of love. No…not really. How about you?"

"I was once in love with a man that I hated." She answered.

They finished breakfast and hit the road. As they drove, Marcia read his notebooks. She had asked him to bring them along. She explained that, if he really felt that he was a writer, he shouldn't be afraid to let an editor see what he did. It felt odd, being so open, letting her read his thoughts. Yet, he liked the fact that this allowed her to get to know him. If she couldn't care for him as he really was, it would be best to discover it early on.

They were making good time and probably could have made it to New Orleans in the early morning hours. They were not expected until the next day however, so they drove and talked about love and sex until late in the night, when they found another motel room a hundred miles from their destination.

They walked to the motel office and went inside. There was no one there, but the bell on the door rang and they could hear a television in the next room. An old man walked out and gave them a smile as he walked to the counter.

"How you folks doing tonight?" He asked.

"A little tired from the drive." Brad told him. "But otherwise, very well."

"What you two need is a little entertainment." He offered, then turned and yelled into the other room. "Harriet, there's a couple here who need some comic relief!"

"Actually, we just need a room for the night..." Marcia started. Harriet appeared then, carrying a small red dog in a blue hat.

"This is my wife Harriet and this is our dog Snickers." The old man said, taking the dog and setting him on the counter. Snickers sat down and looked at Brad and Marcia.

"He was a circus dog, but now he's retired and lives with us." Harriet explained. "We don't know why his fur is so red, but we'll admit to putting the hat on him."

Brad and Marcia assumed that seeing the dog was the entertainment, so they smiled and said that he was cute.

"He's more than just a pretty face." The old man told them. "He's the most intelligent dog in the whole world. At least, that's what he told us."

"He talks?" Marcia asked. It seemed a mistake to encourage them, although it did seem amusing to her.

"He sure does." Harriet said. She turned to the dog. "Would you like a snack Snickers? What would you like?…"

"Popcorn." Snickers said.

Marcia and Brad looked at each other. They had both heard the dog say it. Harriet left the office for a moment, then returned with a bag of popcorn. She opened it up and set it down in front of the Snickers. The dog took his paw, removed a piece of popcorn and tossed it into his mouth.

"That's amazing." Marcia said.

"He's an amazing dog." The old man nodded. "Do you two have a dog?"

"No." Brad told him.

"Well, you've got to get yourself a dog." He said.

"What else does he say?" Marcia asked.

"Oh, he's quite a talker." Harriet told them. "Sometimes he gets to talking and he just won't shut up…"

Snickers turned and looked at her for a moment, then put his paw back in the bag and tossed a kernel of popcorn into his mouth.

"Since he's retired, he doesn't really like to perform for strangers though."

As Snickers sat on the counter, tossing popcorn into his mouth, Brad and Marcia filled out the registration card and got the key to the room. They thanked the old couple for the entertainment and started out.

"Goodnight." Snickers said.

The room was small and the bed was big. A painting of Snickers hung above it. Marcia and Brad made love, then fell asleep exhausted. Brad woke up in the night, feeling quite happy to be in bed with her, yet wondering if it might all be temporary. He knew that it was possible Marcia would leave his life as quickly as she had entered. He was surprised to find that his concern about this was greater than his fear of facing voodoo kidnappers.

An Aspect of Life

Leonard Ellison awoke in the early morning hours, worried about Brad. He had stopped by the Historical Society with Marcia, offering a brief explanation for his trip; it having to do with voodoo kidnappers. He told himself that he shouldn't worry, that his friend was a smart young man and would do just fine. Putting Brad out of his mind, he found that he was having trouble breathing. He tried to get up, struggled a bit and gave up.

Christine Roberts kneeled beside his bed. She was as young and beautiful as the last day he saw her.

"It's okay Leonard." She said. "I'm here and I'm going to stay with you."

Leonard Ellison felt himself a foolish old man, but found that he too appeared younger. He was as he had been, those mornings long ago, when he would wait for her to walk by his family house. They were bathed in a white glow, which seemed to emanate from a corner of the room.

"I'll love your forever." She said, as he got up and embraced her.

The South Woods

The instructions, as given to Sarah Mitchell, were as follows: They were to drive to New Orleans, where they were to check into a particular hotel. Once there, they would be contacted by one of the voodoo people. When they actually arrived at this particular hotel, they found a message to sit tight until they received a telephone call. They checked in and went out on the balcony to sit. Brad was tense and it was apparent that Marcia was suddenly frightened a bit. They didn't know what to expect.

They'd been there an hour, when they received a telephone call.

"Yeah, this is Jimmy." Came the voice on the line. "I'll be there in a few hours and we'll talk…okay?"

"Sure, okay." Brad said. He and Marcia decided to go out and get a bite to eat. They would return, meet with Jimmy and either find their lives in danger or find Lenny Mitchell and take him home. It was hard to be relaxed enough to eat, with all of the turmoil, yet they'd heard that the food in New Orleans was particularly good.

Once out on the street, they weren't sure where to go to eat. Without being a local, it seemed that it would be difficult to know the great places from the really bad ones. They ended up at a small cafe, where they sat very close, and talked very little.

When they returned to the hotel they found Jimmy Snakespirit waiting in the lobby for them.

He walked over and shook Brad's hand. He seemed to be an okay guy. Then again, he was involved in the kidnapping of Brad's father.

"So, what's going on?" Brad asked.

"Let's go have a drink." Jimmy said. "I'll explain it all to you and we'll be done with this whole thing."

They went to a sleazy bar, where all of the customers looked as though they'd had terribly rough lives. Marcia and Brad were doing their best to play along with the whole situation and act as though everything was normal and under control. They'd decided upon this strategy at the cafe and it seemed to be working just fine. No one paid attention to them at the bar, as they sat and listened to Jimmy's story. Strangely enough, he sounded quite sincere. Jimmy Snakespirit told them the story of his life as they sat there. Brad considered that Jimmy's family was perhaps even more odd than his own and found this comforting.

Jimmy Snakespirit was born into a family known for gifts of prophecy and medicines, as well as the arts. His Grandma delivered him, and held the crying child a long time in her arms, reading his future.

"He has two gifts." She explained, passing the baby to his mother.

"Two gifts?..." His mother asked, as she smiled and held the baby close. "I've never heard of such a thing."

"Oh it happens." The old woman knelt down to look at her grandson. "Problem is that no one can keep two gifts...it's bad luck. But don't you worry...there's a way to remedy the situation."

"How?" Wanda asked.

"A ceremony." She explained. "We'll do it when he comes of age and comes into his powers. We'll find someone deserving and give them the lesser gift."

The problem was determining which was the gift that would best be kept. Looking at his hands and eyes, she read that he would be a painter. Yet, he had the gift of prophecy as well. Being as other members of the family could do readings and tell fortunes, it seemed best that he be a painter. Financial potential was to be considered, as each family member used their gift to earn a living for the greater good of them all.

Grandmother knew something else about the boy, which she kept to herself. He would be famous for a time and be written about in the newspapers and talked about on television. His story would eventually be told in a book and preserved for all history.

A gift usually came into power as one reached adolescence. Grandma Snakespirit believed that the excess gift had to be passed on to another in the child's thirteenth year and it would be best if the gift was shared with someone the same age. When they found the family staying in the small Louisiana town that night, the timing was perfect. It was a fairly simple ceremony, compared to some of the others. All that was required was for the gift giver's mother to take a lock of the young man's hair and for her to seduce the father.

Once Brad was chosen to receive the excess gift, his family was invited to the party. Once there, drinks were served, and Jimmy Snakespirit's mother began to dance. She made her way over to Brad, who was staring and smiling, and pulled at his hair. Others joined in the dance.

Lenny Mitchell went off to get another beer. After a time, when he hadn't returned, his wife frowned and climbed to her feet.

"I think it's time for bed." Sarah Mitchell told the boys. They got up and started out.

"Wow…That was great." Brad told his little brother, as their mother ushered them toward their room for the night. She didn't like this place. She sensed that it was unholy and she was anxious to leave as early in the morning as possible. She hoped that her husband wouldn't stay out too late.

The second gift wasn't transferred completely and was weak. It would only come into use in a particular way. Brad could learn of experiences of the deceased, while holding a piece of paper which they had written upon. Jimmy Snakespirit retained part of the ability of prophecy, which found it's way into his paintings.

"We've been blessed!" Wanda exclaimed. "Paintings that can tell fortunes…they will bring top dollar."

"I'm not so sure that it's good." Her mother answered. "It may be a bad sign. Perhaps it was wrong to attempt to create a gifted white man."

"Well, imagine that poor boy…" Wanda laughed. "Can you imagine only being able to tell dead people their fortunes? How many customers will he have?"

Jimmy Snakespirit told them the story of his life as they sat there. He talked about his paintings. Each told a story in a simple, direct style, in bright colors. Only Grandma Snakespirit, as she was called by those who paid her for potions, could interpret his paintings. She would explain the story in each to Jimmy, who couldn't understand them himself. It was her conviction that each one told the story of the person who would come to own it…that each one told the story of the events that would take place in the home where the painting hung.

The ones which offered a happy life were sold as good luck paintings. The ones which predicted trouble were burnt the evening they were painted. This bothered Jimmy terribly, as he often worked hard on them. Yet he believed what his Grandmother had told him and he did so without argument.

The paintings were sold to tourists and locals for years, until one day William Price came to visit. He was from a New York Gallery, and was willing to pay a healthy amount of money for them. When he encountered Jimmy's "bad luck paintings", he was convinced that they were the stronger body of work.

"I don't believe in all this negative magic like you and your family." William Price explained. "And if I don't believe in it, then it has no hold on me. The people who buy these paintings won't know about it…so it won't affect them at all."

Grandma Snakespirit told Jimmy that it was wrong, but he agreed to sell the paintings to the dealer for exhibition in New York. Within a very short period of time, he gained critical acclaim and demand for the paintings grew. The dealer had traveled back often, the amount he would pay for the paintings growing ever greater. Soon, Jimmy was discovered by the media and he was interviewed by a morning news show.

"Funny thing…these painting were supposed to bring so much bad, and they're bringing so much good." He told the interviewer. He had ceased to take his grandmother seriously and talked extensively about his gift and the curse that would supposedly come upon those who purchased certain paintings. The producers thought it a wonderful human interest piece; the story of a true American primitive artist.

The public loved it and articles in major magazines and appearances on late night talk shows followed. Soon, the prices on his paintings reached five figures and they were collected Internationally. The New York dealer, so overcome with this success, had forgotten what he said when he first acquired the paintings; that people wouldn't be affected if they didn't know about the curse. Even if he had, by this time it was too late.

The way it worked was that people would begin to experience bad luck from the time they came into possession of both the work and knowledge of the curse. After this time, bad luck would increase slowly. Those who purchased a painting earlier and for less money would notice the trend sooner and get rid of it. The more a person paid, the less willing they would be to part with the painting and the worse would be their fates. Of course, the fate of each person was encoded within the painting, but not obvious to the owner.

One collector was killed by the painting itself, in a freak accident. He was standing by an open window in his penthouse apartment, when a large gust of wind came up. It blew the painting off the wall and across the room, where it hit him in the head and sent him falling to the pavement. Aside from the couple who were killed by spontaneous combustion, most of the deaths appeared accidental. Still, investigative reporters on evening news teams began to build a scandal. Suddenly, owning a painting by Jimmy Snakespirit was as popular as living in a haunted house and being possessed by a demon.

"What should we do now?" Wanda Snakespirit asked, during a family meeting. Jimmy sat quietly in a corner, not wanting to be glared and growled at.

The old women were in agreement. This gift had to be disposed of. And the only way to do this would be a ceremony, with the original receiver of the gift brought back together with Jimmy. It wouldn't be dangerous to either of them. Jimmy would receive the gift of prophecy and his ability to paint would be eliminated. The other young man would head for home and his ordinary life.

"So, all that we have to do is go through this ceremony, and everything will be alright." Jimmy explained.

Marcia looked at Brad, as he sat considering how it all fit together. Not only had they found an explanation for the gift which had so effected his life and now Marcia's, but they found that his life had long been intertwined with Jimmy's.

"What if Brad likes having this gift." Marcia asked, being something of a negotiator.

"For me, the gift is the way I support my family...it represents our livelihood here." He explained, turning to Brad. "How important is it to you?"

"Well, I've found some use for it anyway..." He started to say, then considered that it might be best not to tell him everything. "It made an impression on Marcia."

"Oh..." Jimmy leaned back in his chair, smiling at them. "So having the gift has been a blessing to you?"

"I'd like to go and see my father."

"Sure...C'mon."

They followed Jimmy outside and to his car. They all climbed in and Jimmy drove. The three of them passed through a very good neighborhood and a very bad neighborhood, then into an industrial area, then into the country. An hour later they drove down a couple of dirt roads, eventually pulling into a clearing in the woods. Here, a couple of old beat up houses sat on a hill behind a group of broken down recreational vehicles.

They followed Jimmy up to one of the houses and inside. There Brad found his father, sitting on a sofa with a woman. They were both naked and he had a beer in his hand. They glanced up from the television as they came in and it took a moment for Lenny Mitchell to recognize his son; to realize that he was actually there staring at him. They grabbed a blanket from the back of the sofa and covered themselves up.

"Brad...What are you doing here?" Lenny Mitchell asked.

"What do you mean?"

"Well, how did you know that I was here."

"Mom told me."

"Your mother knows that I'm here?"

"Sure..." Something was wrong, Brad thought, his father seemed quite comfortable and content in these strange surroundings. "She told me that you had been kidnapped."

"Kidnapped?"

"I'm sorry. It's all my fault." Jimmy stepped forward.

"What?" Lenny Mitchell seemed to be quite surprised by all of it. He turned to face the woman. "What's going on?"

"Who's she?" Brad asked, the intimacy between her and his father quite apparent.

"Oh, this is Wanda...Jimmy's mother."

"Hello." Wanda smiled and nodded, nervously. "Could you all leave us alone for a moment. I need to explain something to your Father."

"Uh, yeah, sure..." Brad stammered. It was all very confusing. As much as he wanted to hear Wanda's explanation, he wanted a moment to try to come to grips with it all himself. Suddenly, Brad remembered his manners. "Oh, this is Marcia."

Lenny Mitchell and Wanda Snakespirit both said hello, then the three walked outside.

"Your mother and my father are friends?" Brad asked Jimmy once they were a few yards from the house.

"Yes." He said. "I'll explain. Your father wasn't kidnapped. We're not bad people. My mother and your father...they've been having an affair for a long time. He was down here visiting...and we needed to get you to come down."

"Does father know about the gift?...Does he know what's going on?"

Lenny Mitchell walked out of the house then. Fastening his pants, he started toward them.

"I think that he knows exactly what's going on now." Jimmy said. "I'll leave you to talk to each other."

As Lenny Mitchell passed Jimmy, he smiled faintly and nodded. Brad knew that he was going to want him to surrender his gift and go through the ceremony.

"So, how are you son?" Lenny Mitchell asked.

"I'm not sure. I don't know what's worse, having my mother tell me that my father has been kidnapped, or finding him sitting naked in a slummy little house with some sort of voodoo woman."

"Come now son...you're old enough now that you can handle all of this."

Lenny Mitchell turned to Marcia. "So young lady, are you Brad's new girlfriend?"

"Yes." Marcia said, stopping Brad's thought processes dead in their tracks. He liked her and liked the idea that she saw herself as his girlfriend.

"You've got good taste, son."

"Don't change the subject." Brad said, coming back around to his senses. "What is going on here?"

"Well, it's a long story..." Lenny Mitchell hesitated, then realizing that Brad was willing to listen to all of it, continued. "Back when you were little, we took a trip. Do you remember, the time we went to Gettysburg and traveled down through the Appalachian Mountains?"

"Yeah."

"Well, that's when I first met Wanda, and Jimmy. You two are the same age you know..."

Brad listened as Lenny Mitchell told his version of the story.

"And you let me become part of this voodoo ceremony?"

"No...I didn't know about it when it happened. Wanda told me years later."

"But you know that they want me to go through another ceremony?"

"Yeah, well, they've had a terrible run of luck, you know." Lenny Mitchell started toward the house. "Let's get inside, the mosquitoes out here are eating me up."

The three of them walked back inside. Lenny Mitchell sat down beside Wanda. Jimmy was sitting cross legged on the floor. Marcia and Brad stood there. It seemed to Brad that everyone was staring at him, apparently awaiting his answer.

"Marcia and I need to go for a little walk and talk." Brad explained. They turned and walked back outside.

"What do you think?" Brad asked.

"What do you think?"

"Well, I don't know what to think."

"Well, I certainly don't have any idea what to think of all this..."

They walked along, and didn't say anything for a moment.

"You sort of feel for them don't you...that the gift belongs to them." She said finally.

"Yeah." Brad nodded.

"So, tell me...Do you know exactly where everything is buried in the corn field? Will you need the gift to guide you?"

"No, I already know where it is."

Brad and Marcia stood there and looked at each other and it was apparent that they were in agreement.

"Okay, let's do the ceremony." He said, as they walked back into the house.

Lenny Mitchell and Wanda Snakespirit smiled and looked at each other. Jimmy walked over and shook Brad's hand. Brad knew that it meant a great deal to the man he had just met, who's life he had been tangled up in for so many years.

The locals all came for the ceremony. It seemed that everyone knew that the Snakespirit clan always put on a great party, and that there would be drink and food for all. Aside from this, there was the usual attraction of voodoo dancing, scantily clad bodies and an element of danger.

Brad could remember a little of the ceremony that he'd been part of two decades earlier. It was suggested that they imbibe; that it would all go better if they were able to get into the spirit of it all. Marcia and Brad watched each other the whole time. It seemed to Brad that she was worried about him and he liked the look in her eyes.

The ceremony wasn't terribly complicated, except for the way it affected Lenny Mitchell's relationship with Wanda. It seemed that, over the years, they had fallen in love. The ceremony represented reversal and, as part of it, they had to end their relationship. Just as he was originally seduced, now he had to say goodbye. As is often the case, love took the backseat to economics, and Wanda Snakespirit took it all in stride, seeing her son Jimmy receive his gift and means of income. Lenny Mitchell felt bad about his son seeing it all as a betrayal to his mother, so he was willing to say goodbye. An attempt to put it all behind them and get their lives straightened out was in order.

Jimmy Snakespirit received his gift in full and a great deal of his talent for painting was transferred to Brad, who hadn't been aware that it was part of the arrangement. Wanda Snakespirit and her mother (who performed the ceremony) assured Brad that, as he had no longer had any gift for prophecy, he would paint neither good or bad luck art. They would be very expressive, ordinary paintings.

Going Home

After the ceremony, Lenny Mitchell asked if he could ride back with Brad and Marcia. Wanda Snakespirit wanted to make him breakfast and they wanted to talk. They made plans to leave at 9 am. Brad knew that they wanted to say their good-byes and, although he hadn't gotten over the feeling that his father had betrayed his family, he understood that it meant a great deal to them.

Brad stayed up late talking with Jimmy. He found that it bothered Jimmy terribly that people had actually died because of his paintings. This was one of the reasons he so appreciated Brad's going through the ceremony, so that he would be guaranteed that he would never paint another one of the "bad luck paintings".

Brad was happy that he could help and he was happy to have lost his gift. He would enter into a life that was more ordinary. Yet his life would be different and that could be a bit frightening. Jimmy and Brad got along very well. Although they planned to continue living their lives quite a distance from each other, felt they would always be friends. They shared a bottle of whiskey and partied until sunrise.

Brad woke up a few hours later feeling horrible.

"You're a little green around the gills." Lenny Mitchell told him. Brad walked out in the woods and vomited twice. He stood against a tree for a time and started to feel better.

"You don't drink often, do you?" Marcia asked, wiping his head with a wet towel. "I mean, it's just that you don't seem cut out for it."

She was right, he had never been able to keep up with the people he knew and went out drinking with. He usually enjoyed a couple of drinks, then went home and slept. He'd been quite a party animal as a teenager, running wild with Randy, but was no longer able to do it.

Once Brad was feeling better, Jimmy took him and Marcia into the woods and showed them his tree house. There were photographs of paintings on the walls and a poster announcing his first exhibition at the Werner/Price Gallery. Brad looked around this place which Jimmy called home and out the window into the woods. It was strange how similar their lives were and yet their worlds were so very different.

"The photos are of a few of my favorite paintings, even though some of them were bad luck paintings." Jimmy explained. "Grandma did a reading and found that there was no magic in the photos, so it's safe to keep them around."

Marcia walked over and stood in front of one of the photos. Brad walked over behind her.

"Oh, yes…that one. It was a good luck painting." Jimmy said. "And now I know what it means."

Marcia and Brad recognized the couple. Even though it was a rather poor photograph of an impressionistic image, they saw themselves.

"Where is this painting now?" Brad asked.

"I sold it to the New York Gallery and who knows who they sold it to."

They stood looking at the photo for a moment, then turned and told Jimmy that they should be heading home. They walked down the hill together and again Brad was struck by the similarity of their daily lives. The woods of Louisiana were decidedly different than those of the North Woods, yet there were so many parallels.

Lenny Mitchell was outside and had placed his suitcase beside the car. He was looking at Wanda, who was standing in the doorway, some distance from him. It seemed that they were trying to get used to being apart from each other a little at a time. Brad thought it was very much like the way he walked out into the lake water the first time every summer…allowing each part of himself to adjust to the shock of the cold a bit at a time.

Brad handed his father the keys. Lenny Mitchell slowly put his suitcase in the trunk, then walked around the car and got in the back seat.

"It was nice to meet you." Marcia told Jimmy, as she turned and started toward the car. It seemed that she wasn't sure what to make of the whole situation. She had fallen asleep and hadn't spent the time with Jimmy that Brad had. She wasn't as comfortable with him as he was.

"I'm glad I got to meet you." Jimmy said. She smiled and got in the car.

Jimmy and Brad stood there and looked at each other. Brad felt that they would meet again and didn't feel they were saying goodbye.

"I hope that you know how much I appreciate your doing this." Jimmy said. "I mean, going through the ceremony and giving up your gift…it was a lot to ask, I know."

"Yeah." Brad nodded. "I'm glad that I could help."

"I can't really ever pay you back, but now that I have the gift I can see the future…If you want to know."

Brad nodded and Jimmy leaned forward, lowering his voice.

"Marcia is the woman you'll spent the rest of your life with…" He explained. "…And you'll be happy together."

Brad shook his hand and thanked him. Once they were on the road, Marcia asked him what Jimmy had said. Brad wouldn't say and he tried not to smile, but his heart was beating wildly.

Lenny Mitchell sat in the back seat, drinking quietly from a bottle, on the way home. The liquid smelled terrible and wasn't his usual brand. He explained that it was an herbal remedy that Grandma Snakespirit had made for him, to assist him in forgetting. It was his intention to go home and be a good husband. He spent a great deal of the trip asleep.

"So, tell me Brad Mitchell. What do you want to be when you grow up?"

Brad looked at Marcia for a moment, then returned his attention to the highway.

"I'm in my thirties. I think that I am grown up."

Marcia was concerned that she had insulted him, which hadn't been her intention.

"What I mean to ask is, what are you going to do with the rest of your life?"

"Pretty much what I've done with this much of my life." He sounded a bit defensive to her. "It's worked for me so far."

"But if you could do anything you want with your life…" She paused, realizing that, as far as Brad was concerned, he was doing what he wanted with his life. "What if you had enough money to change your life anyway you wanted and spend more time doing what you wanted?"

"Well, I would do the same thing as the next guy, I think…I would quit my job."

"And what would you do with the extra time?"

"I would write."

Marcia had been reading Brad's notebooks and didn't doubt that he probably had some sort of undeveloped literary gift.

"What would you write about?" She asked.

"Same thing I write about now." He answered.

The thought which came to her mind had to be worded gingerly. "Um, I like what I've read of your writing…but I've got to say that, in a sense, nothing really happens in your stories."

"That's because they're mostly true and nothing ever happens in the North Woods."

"Yes, but to make it as a writer, you need to create something that moves along at a certain clip…"

Brad was quiet and watched the highway ahead.

"You found my writing boring." Brad said, finally.

"No, it's not that…it's just that nothing happens and people like to read books where something happens."

"I'll take that into consideration." Brad told her.

Home

When they arrived back in the North Woods, Sarah Mitchell and Aunt Jane were happy to learn that everything was alright and that Lenny was safe. Brad changed the story a bit, as there was no reason to talk about his father's relationship with Wanda Snakespirit. Lenny and Sarah Mitchell went for a walk, as they felt they needed to discuss it all. Everyone seemed to feel pretty good about the situation; the men in the family had returned from their adventure safely.

When Tina and the baby came home, Brad sat and played with the baby for awhile. Marcia had gone back to her house. They planned to meet in the corn field at midnight.

Brad carried the baby into the kitchen, where Tina was washing dishes.

"How is everything?" He asked.

"Fine." She seemed happy to see him, but a little angry at the same time.

"How's Charlie?"

"He's okay...still making it with your girlfriend's sister." Now, it was apparent that she was a little upset.

"You're not jealous about Charlie and Cyndi are you?"

"No, not about them…" Tina turned to face him. "It has to do with you and Marcia."

"I thought you liked her..." Brad started, as it all became apparent to him. Tina and he had been spending a lot of time together and had become close. He had never considered that they would become intimate, but now he suspected that Tina had.

"She's nice." Tina turned to him and smiled. "But you know how much I like you...and the baby likes you..."

"And you know how much I like you." He tried to put it all into his voice. To say that she should know that he liked her, but not in that manner.

She nodded and smiled and it seemed that she understood. He walked over to kiss her gently on the cheek. She turned, so that his lips were upon hers. She pressed herself against him and he pulled away. Neither of them moved or spoke for a moment, then she nodded and smiled again.

"I just went through a voodoo ceremony." He explained, to take the edge off of the situation. "I guess that I still have some sort of animal magnetism in me."

Brad walked away and out of the room, shocked and embarrassed and hurting to know that someone he loved was hurting. Tina had come to feel that it might have worked out differently between them. He liked her very much, but knew that Marcia and he would marry. He'd felt it from the beginning and Jimmy Snakespirit had confirmed it.

Lenny and Sarah Mitchell walked down the road together, not saying anything. He reached out and took her hand. She tried to remember the last time they had held hands and the memories went back decades. Their children were babies and the world was all she'd envisioned growing up; a magical, romantic place.

"Seems like I've been out on the road a long time." Lenny Mitchell said finally.

"Just tell me that you've really come home to me." Sarah said. She stopped walking, feeling that perhaps she couldn't go on.

"I've come home." He said.

He smiled and squeezed her hand.

"I was so proud of Brad." She told him, as they continued down the road. "The way he took the responsibility of taking care of the family upon himself…"

"He's a good boy." Lenny Mitchell said. "I'm proud of him to…and I hope that I can make him proud of me again."

Sarah Mitchell stood and looked at her husband. He was home and that brought her as much joy as she had ever hoped for. Yet, her heart was heavy, as there was something left undone.

"I need to have a talk with Brad about something…" She said. "And I'm not looking forward to it."

Brad walked out of the kitchen and found his mother and father standing by the door.

"Brad, I need to talk with you a minute." His mother said, as she led him out on to the porch.

"What is it?"

"I was looking for the right time, or the right way to tell you…" She sat down on the porch swing, and looked down at her hands. "It's about old Mr. Ellison." She paused and took a deep breath. "He died in his sleep the day you went to get your father."

Sarah Mitchell looked at her son as the shock came upon his face. He was feeling as though he'd been hit in the head, suddenly dazed and aching. She walked over and took him in her arms.

"There wasn't a funeral. He didn't really have any friends or family living. They've already buried him. He was an old man you know, and he had a good, long life…"

It was true, Brad thought. He didn't doubt that Mr. Ellison was happy on the other side.

"I wish I had my gift again..." Brad said. "If only for a moment...so that I could say goodbye."

Mother went into the house and he stood there for awhile, staring down the road. The thought kept running around in his head; he would never see Mr. Ellison again.

The plan, as developed by Marcia, had the two of them going to their own homes after dinner and meeting at midnight in the cornfield to do the dig. Storm clouds had gathered by the time they sat down for dinner however and rain began to fall. Marcia drove to the Mitchell house at ten o'clock and they stood on the porch, looking out at the pouring rain. As much as she hated doing it, she admitted that they had to postpone the dig. Brad suggested that she stay the night, as he had already grown accustomed to sleeping with her. They walked together under an umbrella, up the trail to his treehouse.

"So, Marcia seems pretty cool." Randy and Brad were sitting on the porch together.

"Yeah, she is."

"I knew that you'd find someone like her...She was every-where in your old notebooks—in the poems and everything."

"Yeah, I guess that's true." It came to Brad's mind that Randy was dead. He wasn't supposed to have any trace of the gift and didn't know how their conversation was taking place. Randy didn't seem concerned, or aware that he was no longer living. It seemed to Brad that he shouldn't mention it, but he did.

"Why are you here?" He asked after a moment. "You're dead."

"Yeah, well you're not really here either." Randy said. "It happens to people. They meet up with dead friends in their dreams. It's an ordinary experience."

They laughed together. Randy had often joked about Brad being an ordinary guy and that's what he was learning to be.

For over twenty years Brad had the gift and during that time, as far as he knew, he did not dream. It was not until he began to paint that he began to have vivid dreams and realized that they had long been missing. The dreams of childhood which he did remember, monsters and experiences with his family and friends had been difficult to differentiate from memories.

"Was there a time when we went out fishing in a little boat and got caught in a tremendous storm?" He would ask his mother.

"No. I don't think so." She would say. "Unless your father took you out and I didn't know about it."

"Was there a time when I was chased through the woods by a giant furry creature?"

"Oh yes, I remember that. You were five and were playing out back and you suddenly came running up to the porch and told us what had happened. We didn't see the creature, but you insisted that it had been out there."

Brad came to the conclusion that it would be difficult to separate his early dreams and experiences from each other in his mind and that it was all best left as it was.

The next morning, Brad left Marcia sleeping in his bed and walked down the hill. He planned on arriving back with coffee, muffins and a bouquet of flowers before she woke up.

"You got a call. Long distance, from Los Angeles..." Sarah Mitchell said, as he walked into the house.

"Oh." Randy would call occasionally and for a moment Brad was confused that she was saying that it had been him. He stood there a moment and his mother noticed the expression on his face.

"It was a girl named Lorna. She said you might not remember her…She said that she was Randy's girlfriend. She wants you to call her back. The number is next to the phone."

"Thanks." Brad said, going off to the telephone. He remembered meeting Lorna when she had flown back for Randy's funeral.

Brad dialed the number and listened to the ringing.

"Hello?" Came a girl's voice.

"Hi, Lorna?" Brad asked.

"No, this is Hillary…hold on."

She sat the phone down and Brad listened to the music that they had on. It was a song from the seventies by Seals & Crofts.

"Hi, this is Lorna." Came a voice, a few minutes later.

"Hi. This is Brad Mitchell."

"Oh, hi. How are you?"

"Pretty well. How are you doing?"

"Well, you know, Randy dying and everything threw me for a loop…but I'm doing better now. You know, getting on with my life…"

"Yeah. I know what you mean."

"I called you because I recently moved out of the bungalow Randy and I lived in. I'm sharing an apartment with someone and I really have no room. And, you know, I still have boxes of Randy's stuff…"

"What stuff?"

"Well, I gave all of the valuable stuff to his family after it happened. You know, his guitars and musical equipment…but I wasn't ready at that point to part with all of the tapes and his notebooks. I'd like to send you all of it and then you can talk to his parents and share it with them."

"Why send it to me first?"

"I'd like for you to hear the songs, especially the mixes of the ones he was working on when it happened. Randy told me quite a bit about the songs…about you and the lyrics…

"Yeah?"

"You know, he was working on a musical when he died. He said that the two of you had written all of these songs together and that a lot of them were about you and your family."

"Yeah." Brad said, unable to say anything else. He supposed that he wasn't surprised Randy had never gotten the idea of a musical out of his head.

"That's why I felt I should send you everything first." Lorna said.

"Thanks. I appreciate it."

Brad and Lorna chatted for a moment, although neither of them were able to say too much about Randy. Brad figured that they would talk again, after more time had passed and share stories.

The following afternoon, the rain let up a bit. Marcia wanted to spend some time with Cyndi, so Brad dropped her off at home and drove down to the Historical Society. Once there, he sat on the steps, thinking it all over. One of the reasons he had never left his home town was that he liked for life to move very slowly. Suddenly, everything was happening so fast; people came into his life and others left forever. He wanted time to go into himself for awhile and roll all the people and events around in his head, to see how it all fit. Yet, he worried that he might sink into a melancholy from which he might never escape. Because of Marcia, Brad wanted to stay in the world, with his feet on the ground, and carry on.

A large black Buick pulled into the drive and the Mayor got out. His name was William Peterson and he was one of Aunt Jane's old boyfriends.

"Hey Brad…" He said, approaching and shaking Brad's hand. The Mayor climbed the steps. He pulled a set of keys out of his pocket and opened the door, gesturing for Brad to follow him inside. It seemed odd to Brad, seeing someone walking into the Historical Society; to think about going in with Mr. Ellison gone. Brad had suspected that someone would come along to take care of the place and supposed that the Mayor had as much right as anyone. Brad went in to find him sitting at Mr. Ellison's desk.

"I'm here to fulfill one of my responsibilities as Mayor, although I'm here as a friend more than anything. Fact of the matter is that I don't really have any responsibilities as Mayor of this little town…" He glanced around the room as he spoke, nodding his head and smiling. "But just as Mr. Ellison felt the need to look after this place, I've always felt the need to look after the town."

William Peterson took an envelope out of his pocket, looked at it for a moment, then held it out for Brad to take.

"What's this?" He asked, receiving it.

"Well, I was also Mr. Ellison's attorney and he had a will. You're in it."

"I am?" Brad held the envelope and tried to imagine what possessions Mr. Ellison might have.

"He didn't really have any family and he was very fond of you Brad. He left you just about all of it, aside from the cabin and his boat, which he willed to the town. Although, I'm not sure what we'll do with them…"

"What did he leave to me?" Brad asked.

"Read it." William Peterson said. "There's a copy of the will inside and a letter for you.

Brad opened the envelope. He set the will aside and read the handwritten letter:

Brad,

I want to thank you for being a great friend and a decent chess opponent. I certainly never expected to live so long and you made my life worth living right up until the end. Perhaps the greatest aspect of your gift is the knowledge that the dead live. I always found great comfort in that, just as you can be assured that I'm not really gone and that we'll meet again.

I must apologize that I wasn't ever totally honest with you in regard to the Historical Society. I probably should have told you that I owned it and that a town the size of ours couldn't afford the upkeep of such a place. I had hoped that you might come to see the importance of the place over the years.

Having lived so long, I've seen the progression of machines and all that is called progress, and I've noticed that men have allowed their souls to slip away. I believe that the Historical Society has the answers...the stories that could make our country a wonderful place once again. The people I've known in my lifetime, the immigrants and children of immigrants...here are their photos, letters and journals. They explain the joy and great sense of freedom they experienced. Freedom to work, worship and own property were worth all of the hardships this land offered. People can learn so much from the histories of these people...they can come to know what it is they have. That we have each been given a great gift.

I realize that you are a young man and it would be wrong for you to pass your time cooped up in this musty old place. You must live, indeed that lesson is to be learned from this place as well. I hope that you'll look after the building though and try to make it available to others. Give it half the time you gave me, that's all I ask. Perhaps, when you're an old man it will pay you back with all of the comfort and joy I found in it.

Your friend,
Leonard Ellison

Brad looked up from the letter, his heart heavy and uplifted.

"I didn't even know his first name until a week ago." Brad said. "His old flame referred to him as Leonard and it seemed so strange."

"His old flame?…"

Brad realized that the story was too long, not to mention unbelievable. Now that the gift was gone, he knew that it would never become public knowledge and that in time the rumors about it would be forgotten.

"He's been around for all of my life." William Peterson said. "I can't imagine this town without him."

"Either can I."

"The Historical Society is yours now…the property, the building and all of it's contents."

Brad nodded.

"What will you do with it?…The real estate is probably worth a fair amount of money."

Brad looked around the room. It was difficult to imagine that Mr. Ellison was gone. In a sense, he felt that his old friend remained there among the books and relics.

"I think that the Historical Society needs to carry on." Brad said.

When he arrived home, Brad found Charlie sitting on the porch, carving patterns into a turned wood bowl.

"What's up?" Brad asked.

"I was just thinking about Cyndi." Charlie said.

"I want to marry her."

"You've got to get divorced."

"Yeah...I know. I wonder how Tina will take it." He seemed genuinely concerned.

"Well, I'm sure that she'll take it pretty well." Brad assured him. "After all, I think that she hates your guts."

"Maybe." Charlie smiled and nodded. "But don't underestimate the power of love...she hasn't really faced the prospect of having to learn to get along without me."

"If you divorce her the court will demand that you pay alimony and child support."

"I know...Cyndi and I discussed it. We feel that it's the right thing to do, even though we'll have to make sacrifices for it."

"Talk to Tina about it." Brad advised him. "I think that she'll be able to handle it."

Leah Sauer was spending every evening at Thomas' penthouse apartment, being the perfect lover. He still hadn't asked her to move in, but she had begun to do so slowly, telling him that she needed certain things if she was going to sleep over and go to work first thing in the morning. She was happy to have all of her cosmetics in the bathroom and each week she managed to bring another half dozen outfits over.

Thomas had brought the painting by Jimmy Snakespirit home and it hung in the dining room. He had wanted to hang it in the bedroom, but Leah managed to convince him not to. It's not that the girl in the painting looked to her like Marcia, but she knew that it did to him. She definitely wanted to keep Marcia out of his bedroom.

Thomas hadn't heard from Marcia in quite a while, and had all but given up on her. His heart had healed easily, but his pride was still smarting. He was convinced that she had found someone else. She had lost her mind, he told himself, moving off to the boondocks to live a hillbilly life. When he came home he found Leah out on the patio sunning herself. She had removed her top and he stood there looking at the way she was stretched out.

He knew that he'd put up with her slowly moving into his place, as long as she continued to turn him on this way.

Marcia and Brad were standing on the porch of the tree house having coffee. It had stopped raining for the moment. Brad knew that, even if it stopped raining completely, the cornfield would still be filled with mud. He wondered how long he could postpone the dig. Tina appeared in the clearing below, walking up the trail to visit. Charlie's talk with her had gone very well and she was coming to tell them about their visiting a lawyer and having papers drawn up. Soon they would be divorced and Tina would be receiving child support checks from him on a regular basis.

Tina had brought along a bag of sweet rolls. Brad poured her a cup of coffee and the three of them sat and talked. He noted that Marcia and Tina seemed to get along very well.

"So, what will you do now?" He asked.

"I don't know." Tina answered. She had been very upbeat about the prospects of her freedom, but now her cheer was hidden. "I don't know where to go."

"So don't go." Marcia said.

"None of us want for you and the baby to move away." Brad told her. "You're family."

"Well, I'd like to stay in town. But you know, I can't stay in the house."

"Yes, of course." Marcia agreed.

They sat and watched a group of squirrels that were playing in a nearby tree.

"Maybe you can build a tree house of your own." Brad suggested. "Or maybe a small cabin if you prefer. The family owns acres of woods back here…"

Tina nodded her head and smiled, although she did not imagine that it would be possible. But then, she imagined if it could be worked out, she and the baby could be truly happy. The three of them discussed it and agreed that they weren't sure how Charlie would like the idea. The next day when Cyndi came over to see Marcia, she brought the subject up to her.

"That would be great." Cyndi said, in all goodness. "I didn't want to be responsible for a situation where Charlie couldn't spend time with his child…this would be great for all of us."

"You wouldn't have any problems with it?" Marcia asked her. "Living so close to his ex-wife?"

"You mean like jealousy?" Cyndi asked. "Heck, if there's one woman in this town that doesn't want Charlie, it's her."

The rain continued, but Sarah and Lenny Mitchell went away for the weekend regardless. They insisted that they would spend the next couple of days in sunshine, though such a place seemed thousands of miles away. Marcia and Brad were together most of the time, as were Charlie and Cyndi. One night, the sisters decided to have dinner at home with their father. Charlie and Brad went into town for pizza. Brad was happy to see that Tim was doing well at the pizzeria. Tim was still thinking that Brad would be back; that he was still on vacation. Brad wasn't so sure. Everything had changed.

Brad and Charlie got a pizza and stopped at the market for beer. They drove down to the waterfront, where they ate and drank and talked about building a cabin for Tina and the baby. Charlie felt that perhaps Tina and the baby should remain in the house and that it was he and Cyndi who should build a home for themselves.

This was the fourth day and it didn't rain at all. Marcia called when they got home to ask if they could meet later and dig. Brad said yes.

The Dig

Brad was there at midnight. He didn't want to be early, as it was all fairly spooky. Yet he wanted to be on time, because he didn't want for Marcia to think that he had chickened out. She was there waiting, with shovels.

"So where is it?" She asked.

He took one of the shovels and led her to the spot. They stood there in silence for a moment, then she dug her shovel into the ground and left it there. She walked over and kissed him hard upon the lips.

"I don't want you to think that..." She started to say, then stopped. "I appreciate your doing this for me...and I, um, want you to know how I feel."

She didn't tell him how she felt. Rather, she walked away, not wanting to look at him. She picked up her shovel and started to dig. Brad didn't know what to think and he definitely didn't know what to say. If she was falling in love with him, and the way she was acting suggested this, he was very happy. If she was leading him on to get his help, she was successful. As he ran it all over in his head, he began to dig.

They dug for hours and were exhausted. Marcia had thought ahead, bringing a blanket, a bottle of white wine and snacks.

They lay on the blanket, resting, for some time. He wasn't sure about her, but he was hoping that they might call it a night.

"Why haven't we hit anything yet?" Marcia asked, after considerable time had passed.

"We have further to go. Back then, times were tougher and so people were tougher." Brad explained. "They buried it very deep."

Marcia rolled over against him, again pressing her mouth against his.

"If you want to call it a night…or if you want out…or if you want to forget the whole thing…I understand." She told him. "I'll still want to be with you."

Brad kissed her, smiled and climbed to his feet.

"Let's dig a little more." He said.

They resumed digging and in less than an hours time, hit something solid.

"I felt that this was the case, but I found it hard to believe." He told her. "It's the roof of the car…they buried the entire car."

This discovery was quite exciting to him, as it confirmed that his original vision had been correct. The bodies would all be stuffed inside the car and the money would be found in the trunk. As they uncovered the car, they figured out which area was the trunk, and were able to dig around it alone, hoping to avoid the dead bodies altogether.

As they uncovered the trunk, it suddenly sprang open. Apparently, it hadn't been shut all the way. Brad and Marcia jumped back, almost out of the hole, then turned. They cautiously leaned forward and looked, as Brad pointed the flashlight. The money was not there.

"What could have happened to it?" Marcia asked.

Brad was baffled and they stood there for a moment not saying anything. He considered the possibilities and had one small hunch. He dug a bit more of the car out. He found that the back door of the car was open and that there was a small tunnel leading out to the left of the vehicle.

"Oh my God…" Marcia said, summing it all up. "One of them wasn't dead…"

Brad wondered if it was possible that someone had actually gotten out of the car, opened the trunk and removed the money. Were they able to dig their way out? Brad and Marcia started to dig in the direction of the tunnel, to find out where it led. They hit something solid, which proved itself to be the remains of a shoe and a foot.

"Wow…bad news for him." Brad said, considering what it must have been like to be so close to living and being rich, then dying such a horrible death. "But hey, it's good news for us."

Brad dug a little further and retrieved a metal box. Marcia climbed up out of the hole and he passed it to her. Once he was out, they opened it. The money was safe and sound. They sat there for a long period of time looking at it.

"What will you do with it?" He asked Marcia.

"Well, I'll have to split it up with my family…with my sister anyway. But I'll still have a fair amount. I'll give you your cut. To tell the truth, I have given it some thought. I think that I want to go into business. I'm tired of working for someone else. I would like to start a small publishing house…"

They were both tired and sweaty. Brad helped Marcia carry the trunk back to her house, where they locked it in the trunk of her car. They agreed to meet at the Pancake House for breakfast in the morning. Having slept on it, they would decide how to proceed.

Brad tossed and turned during the night, going over it all in his head. It came to his mind that Marcia might take the money and go back to New York City. He knew that the money didn't really mean anything to him, as he had always been happy in the North Woods, earning an ordinary income. And then Jimmy's prophecy came back to him and he found that he trusted it. Brad slept with a smile on his face. Marcia and he would spend their lives together.

Blueberry Pancakes

When Brad pulled in, he noticed Marcia's car in the lot. He saw her sitting at a table by the window as he walked to the restaurant door. He was exhausted in his mind and body due to the events of the last week. Yet he felt happy and inspired.

"I saw you pull in, so I ordered for you." Marcia said, as he sat down at the table.

"Thanks. What did you order me?"

"Well, I looked over the menu and saw that all they had was pancakes. I told the waitress that I was waiting for you and she said that you always ordered the ones with blueberries."

"Yeah, I do."

"I could grow accustom to this small town life…" Marcia said. "It does have some perks…I mean, for people to know what you want…"

"…And order it for you." Brad added.

"Here's your coffee Brad." He looked up to see that the waitress was Anne, his cousin's wife's sister.

"I've been thinking…" Marcia said, after a moment. "Would you like to be partners?"

"How do you mean?"

"Well, I know that you write…as a matter of fact, I'll bet that the last few days are all recorded in your journal."

"Yeah." He nodded. "I know that I let you read through my notebooks on the trip...but maybe you really shouldn't be reading my journal anymore. I mean, so much of it's about you now..."

"But I want to read it...I think that we should work on it and turn it into a book."

Brad didn't know how to react. It was his ambition to be a writer, but the events of the last week had been too close to home. He didn't say anything. He just sipped his coffee and waited for his pancakes and a change in the conversation.

"As far as I'm concerned, what we've experienced over the last few days...it would make for a fascinating book or movie." Marcia went on, with no interest in changing the subject. "There's a lot of money in movie rights..."

"Randy wanted to take my poems and turn them into songs, then turn it all into a musical. Did I tell you about that?"

"You did."

"Did I tell you what I thought of the idea?"

"Yes. You did."

Brad imagined his journals turned into a book. He promised Marcia that he would give it some thought.

"About the money..." She said. "I found some papers inside telling the name of the bank that the money came out of. I called and they've been out of business for a long time...I would think that would make the money ours, but I'm going to call a few people in New York and make sure. Lawyers, accountants, people who can tell me how to handle it all."

The pancakes arrived then. Brad had worked up an appetite digging all night and dug in. Marcia watched him for a moment. He shook his head, to indicate that he agreed with her, as he chewed. She smiled and started to eat.

"You ordered the blueberry pancakes too." He said.

"I want to get an idea of what life with you would be like."
Marcia said.

Brad looked around the restaurant and thought about the events of the last week.

"Full of adventure." He said.

The Art Business

William Price entered his townhouse and locked the door behind him. It was almost midnight and he was exhausted. It had been a long day at the gallery, followed by dinner at an incredibly pompous but politically connected collector's home. It had been a struggle to say kind things about his second rate paintings all evening, all of which had been purchased through other galleries.

He needed a drink and went to the bar to pour himself a large brandy. He remembered his father and how he would always heat the brandy over a flame. He had tried to carry on this tradition of his father's for a time. William Price knew the importance of ritual, but had long ago given in to the importance of actually having the drink.

A light was blinking on the answering machine and he went over and pressed the button. It was Brad Mitchell again. He had sent his paintings, along with a letter telling a tale of receiving Jimmy Snakespirit's gift. The paintings were indeed very good and directly in the same style. Yet there was little hope of selling primitive paintings by a white guy from the North Woods. He had sent the paintings back, along with a letter composed by his secretary explaining all of it. There was no reason to return the call.

Jimmy Snakespirit's paintings, on the other hand, would be worth a great deal once the controversy blew over. The belief in voodoo couldn't possibly overshadow the quality and importance of the paintings. When people were ready to buy again, they would be paying even higher prices. And he would be ready.

Carrying the glass of brandy, William Price slowly walked to the basement steps. He took out his keys, unlocked the door and opened it. He flicked on the light switch, and went to take the first step. The darkness remained. He tried the switch again, then realized that the light bulb was burned out. He took a long sip of brandy to steady himself, then reached out in the darkness toward the bulb. He couldn't see it in the darkness, but presumed that it was just a bit out of his reach. He stretched his arm out further, then lost his balance and fell forward. William Price flew for a moment, then landed hard on the cement floor below.

A street light, shining from a small street level window, illuminated a corner of the basement. His body was twisted and he was aware of two things; he was unable to move and the light was getting dimmer. He squinted to see, and could make out the corner of one of the Jimmy Snakespirit paintings, which he had stacked in the corner and covered with a blanket.

"Voodoo..." He said, and he tried to laugh, though frightened by the growing darkness.

It all seemed to fade, until he was some place else, where the walls were covered with bold Italian frescoes and there was a sound like Thelonius Monk playing Chopin in the distance.

His story was told on the third page of the New York Times two days later.

The Book

Marcia and Brad went right to work. As he wrote the story, she edited. Aside from spending time with Marcia, his life was not unlike it was before. It was nice to know that they each had money in the bank. Of course, she had a great deal more, but that was fair.

Any trace of his gift for prophecy was gone, but he had started painting a bit. He thought that his work was very good. It was apparent that Mother and Aunt Jane weren't terribly impressed, yet they would both nod and say that he was very gifted.

Jimmy had given him photos of some of his paintings, explaining that neither good luck or curse was in the photos and that they were safe. All known examples of his work had been destroyed. It was apparent to Brad that he was painting in the same style, doing what had been described as abstract and semi-figurative narrative painting.

Brad had gone as far as contacting Jimmy's ex-dealer in New York, a guy named William Price. He sent him a letter and some of his paintings for consideration. He wrote back that he wasn't interested, but wished him luck and suggested an art dealer he knew in Los Angeles.

"Maybe we can use your paintings as illustrations in the book." Marcia suggested.

Brad decided to call the guy that William Price had told him about. He was supposedly a new guy on the art scene, but was enthusiastic about the art business. It was difficult getting past the girl who answered the phone. It occurred to Brad that the gallery probably received a number of calls from artists and she probably screened them. He decided to tell her that it was in regard to Jimmy Snakespirit.

"The guy who does the killer paintings?" She asked.

"Well, I believe that only some of them bring on death." Brad told her.

She asked him to hold for a moment.

"Hello." Came the art dealer's voice on the line.

"Hi, my name is Brad Mitchell. An art dealer in New York named William Price suggested that I call you."

"He did?…When?"

"Last week."

"He died."

"He did?"

"Yes. Yesterday. Why did he suggest you call me?"

"Well, it's a, um…" What was he to say? That he'd received Jimmy's gift to paint in a voodoo ceremony?

"I was told that you were calling in regard to Jimmy Snakespirit." The dealer said.

"Yes, well…are you familiar with his paintings?"

"Certainly. I was negotiating with Mr. Price to represent him in Los Angeles until, well, you know…Everyone who bought his paintings started dying."

"Actually, it wasn't all the paintings." Brad offered. "Just the bad luck ones."

"Yes, well, I'd heard that. And giving Jimmy the benefit of the doubt, I called and talked to him last week. He says that he's not painting at all now."

"Yes, that's true...Now he's a fortune teller."

"Yes, I guess that's what he was saying...Anyway, what's your story?"

Brad went on and did his best to explain it all. He hadn't realized what a long and complicated story it was until he started to tell it. Indeed, it did seem like enough material for a novel. Brad did his best, briefly explaining what had happened and that they planned on publishing a book and perhaps using the paintings as illustrations. The art dealer told Brad that he should send photos of the paintings and more information about the book.

The next day Brad and Marcia took Polaroid photos of a few of the paintings. William Price had explained that it was not customary to send the actual work. Brad didn't think that the photos did them justice, but decided they would have to do. He started to write a cover letter, to explain it all, to give him the story of how he came to paint and his relationship with Jimmy Snakespirit. Marcia and Brad discussed it. He thought that he should send a few chapters from the book; that it told the story and that would be easier than putting it all in a letter. Marcia felt that it couldn't hurt to have a third party take a look at the book. They decided to send a rough version of it along.

Brad and Marcia drove into Bay Springs and found a copy of the New York Times at the bookstore. The story of William Price was on page three. He had met his fate, falling down the stairs into his basement. When they discovered the body, they also discovered a number of paintings by Jimmy Snakespirit stacked under a blanket. He had put together a large collection of what he considered to be the best work; the *bad luck paintings*.

None of the television stations carried the story. The public had grown tired of hearing about Jimmy Snakespirit. A young Hollywood starlet had recently seduced a young boy and was being sued by his parents for a million dollars. This was the news story everyone watched over dinner.

Brad thought that he should call Jimmy, to see if he'd heard about his ex-dealer and to check on how he was doing.

"I feel really bad about all of it…" Jimmy told him. "You know, I've always thought it best to go through life doing some amount of good and trying not to do any bad."

"But you told me that you had warned him." Brad said.

"Yeah, I did. I figure that it's one thing to want to make a living, but wanting to get make big bucks like that…it can get you in trouble."

Neither of them said anything for a moment. Brad had known Jimmy for such a short period of time and had met him believing him to be a kidnapper. It seemed odd that they got along so well. Brad asked him if he had ceased to dream, now that he had the gift and had lost his inspiration to paint.

"Yes." Jimmy said. "And I miss my dreams so much, that sometimes I want to give up the gift, which is bringing in a nice income. Anyway, the lives of people and their futures…it's all so definite. In dreaming and painting it was all wide open and anything was possible."

Brad no longer had the ability to communicate with the dead, but those who were gone would often come and visit him in his dreams. He would find that Randy and he were seventeen years old again and he would be playing guitar and talking about what his life would be like. Brad was able to stop and visit Mr. Ellison and they would share a candy bar and play a game of chess. The living were there in his dreams as well, along with mysterious happenings and scenes of absolute beauty.

Brad would have been happy to pass all of his time in dreams, if not for the fact that his waking life was just as wonderful. He loved Marcia and they were happy. His family was odd, yet many old wounds were healed and everyone was getting on well. It was Autumn and the air was crisp and the woods were beautiful. Aside from being an artist and living in a treehouse, Brad was an ordinary guy.

Marcia Roberts walked around her family home, gathering the last of her possessions and placing them in a box. She'd been practically living in Brad's treehouse, but now it was going to be official. He hadn't just asked her to move in with him, he'd suggested they get married. She'd told him that she preferred to give it some more time, still she didn't doubt that it would happen. Brad believed in destiny and, although she didn't share his belief, she admitted that she'd known he was the one from the moment they met. She had tried to deny it, but after that first day in the cornfield, it had been a feeling deep in her gut.

She felt that calling Thomas would be the right thing. To tell him that she wouldn't be coming back. He hadn't called for sometime, yet she was convinced that he loved her and deserved an explanation. She walked over to the telephone and dialed his number.

"Hello?" Leah Sauer answered the phone.

Marcia was surprised to hear a woman's voice.

"Is Thomas there?" She asked.

"No, he's not." Leah told her. "Can I take a message?"

"Yes this is Marcia." She said, then paused a moment hearing the silence on the other end. "Who's this?"

"This is Leah."

"Leah?…Leah Sauer?"

"Yeah."

"Hi Leah, how are you?"

"Fine."

"What are you doing there?"

Again there was a silence, then the reply:

"Thomas and I are, um, seeing each other."

"Oh." Marcia was surprised and her ego was a bit bruised. She had been replaced rather quickly and easily it seemed. Then again, she had fallen in love with someone else herself.

"Are you, um...coming back?" Leah asked.

Marcia had known Leah for years. She had worked for a time at the publishing house, but had left to pursue her writing.

"No." Marcia told her. "I've met someone."

Leah didn't say anything, but Marcia knew that she was feeling better about the call and maybe even smiling.

"Nice talking to you, Leah. I don't know if I'll call back. If you want you can tell him for me, okay?"

"Sure." Leah said. "Thanks."

"No problem. Bye."

Having quit his job, Brad spent his days writing and painting. Marcia and he spent a great deal of time together. Soon, they would publish a book and sell it. This would bring some income, but the greater amount would come from the movie rights. Someone would certainly see what a great film their story would make. They would get an advance and perhaps a percentage. Then, they could spend the rest of their lives making personal appearances and would be celebrities. People would want to buy his paintings and perhaps they could publish another book and it would become another film and it would all start over again.

What sort of celebrity they would acquire and how people would view them, lay heavy on their minds. People would know Brad and Marcia's love story and discuss their private thoughts and actions. The book reflected their personal lives and it was a little frightening to share all of that with strangers. And then there was the possibility of a movie. How it turned out would make a big difference in that perception and it would be totally out of their control. A company that wanted to make a family/adventure film could make them look like a contemporary Roy Rodgers and Dale Evans. Someone who wanted to make an erotic/adventure film could make them appear to be like Henry Miller and Anais Nin. Would they enjoy their fame, if the spotlight it cast them in was so out of their control?

"We can't reveal all of this." Brad explained to Marcia, as they sat playing cards at the Old Foster Farm one day. "How would people see my family? They would no doubt seem odd to everyone..."

"You're family is wonderful." She said. "But you are right...it could invade our privacy and create problems." She nodded and thought it over for a moment. "I have an idea. We'll present it as a work of fiction and credit it to a fictional character. What do you say?"

"Sure." Brad said. "Why not."

Could they really pull it off? They had been talking to the art dealer in Los Angeles. He seemed genuinely interested in the book and said that he had some connections there and could assist as a go between in publishing it. They asked if he would be interested in having it published under his name. Would he take credit for the whole thing as an act of his imagination? He could put up any smoke and mirrors that would assist in keeping their identity secret.

"I've been looking at the paintings you sent." He told them, when they called. "They're good and I'd like to represent you. I'd like to get people to look at Jimmy's paintings again as well. I think the book would help."

"You would have to guarantee us that you'll keep the secret though..." Brad explained. "It's really important to us."

"Sure." He said. "It's a great story. I'll take the credit and I'll keep the truth a secret."

When Brad hung up the phone, he walked over to where Marcia was sitting. He kissed her and whispered in her ear. They had a plan.

"What are you thinking about?" Marcia asked Brad one day, as they sat on the porch. She was editing and he was painting.

"Nothing." He said. It's the type of thing people often said. Marcia didn't buy it.

"You were thinking of something." She pressed the issue. "What was it?"

"You won't get mad?"

"Only if we cease to communicate."

"I was thinking about all that we've been through. I was thinking about my falling for you and our dig in the cornfield. I've always thought of myself as an ordinary guy. Maybe it all suggests that perhaps I'm odd...and that I'm following some sort of genetic pattern in my life."

"The problem is that you think that your family is odd."

"The whole town believes that they're odd."

"But they're not. It's like Thoreau said...they hear the beat of a different drummer. Fact is, you're family is wonderful. They're not afraid to be who they are. To pretend not to hear that drummer...that would be wrong. That would be crazy."

"What about mom? She's been such a danger to herself...."

"Yes, but not since your father came back home. She needed a certain kind of love that she was lacking...And, of course, it didn't help that you threw away that device of hers..."

"She was going to take it into the bathtub...She could have been electrocuted..."

"But now everything is okay with your mom and dad...right?"

"Yeah…"

Indeed, it seemed to Brad that his mother and father had been spending more time together and their relationship seemed to have become increasingly physical. His world was beginning to resemble the wonderland he'd experienced as a child.

"But what about Aunt Jane?." He asked. "She seems to be slipping more and more into her private fantasy land…"

"I think that just about everybody has an Aunt like that." Marcia said. "It's just that your Aunt Jane is…a little more free to be who she is."

Brad thought about it. Perhaps there wasn't a great deal of difference between his wonderland and Aunt Jane's fantasy land. Did this make him a little more odd, or her behavior a little more acceptable? It seemed to him that he shouldn't waste time thinking about it. That he should just live.

"You're okay about Charlie and Cyndi?" Brad asked Marcia, after a moment.

"Sure…They love each other. It will be okay." Marcia didn't say anything for a moment, allowing him to consider that everything was indeed going to turn out. "You feel okay about us?"

"I feel great about us." Brad said.

He had never been good about expressing his feelings, and Marcia was very kind in understanding how uncomfortable it made him feel. As he'd answered her and the moment seemed quite heavy, she kindly lightened it up.

"If Charlie and Cyndi get married, we'll be related. We'll be cousins-in-law or something like that, won't we?"

"Yeah." He laughed.

Brad called Jimmy. He knew that they would keep in touch with each other as the years passed and hoped that they would meet again.

"We're writing a book." Brad said.

"Really? What's it about."

"I guess it's sort of autobiographical…it's about my life and the last couple of weeks and everything that happened."

"Really? I'm in it?"

"Yeah, we all are. I don't know…we might change the names. You know, to protect the innocent…and the guilty."

"Yeah, well, as long as you give me a cool name."

"Sure." Brad said. "Listen, I've been painting."

"You're good aren't you."

"Yeah, I think so."

"Yeah, so was I."

"We're thinking about using the paintings as illustrations in the book."

"Good." He said. "You're welcome to use some of mine, if you want."

"Really?…You know, I hadn't thought about it…but you said that there was no magic in the photos of them, right?"

"Yeah, Grandma and I both did a reading of the photos…they're just like photos of normal paintings."

"Really good paintings." Brad added.

"Yeah." Jimmy said.

As caretaker of the Historical Society, Brad continued his habit of stopping by the place on his way to work. Usually, he wouldn't go in. In fact, he felt he needed to become accustom to the place without Mr. Ellison slowly. He would walk around the building, and check to make sure that everything was secure. Marcia and Brad had discussed making the place their office once things started happening. This way he could fulfill his duties and make the place available to everyone. He knew that this would please Mr. Ellison and this pleased him.

Brad and Marcia drove into Bay Springs, and parked next to Joey Lewis' pink hearse. Brad noticed a sign in the window, indicating that it was for sale. Walking up the street, they noticed Joey in the cafe, having lunch with Tina. They walked in and over to the table.

"Hey..." Brad said. "I didn't know that you two knew each other."

"Sure." Joey nodded. "I've been looking at her for years, but you know, she was married to Charlie."

Tina seemed a little embarrassed and it was quite possible that Brad had gone in the cafe for that purpose. She seemed to him like a sister and he felt inclined to tease her. Marcia smiled at her and gave Brad a look to suggest that they leave them alone.

"I noticed that the hearse is for sale." Brad told Joey.

"Yeah. It's just that, I've had it since high school and I guess it's time for a truck or something."

"Or a station wagon..." Brad said, giving Tina a wink and being dragged out by Marcia.

Mary came out of the lingerie shop, as they walked past.

"Hi Brad...Hi Marcia."

"Hello." Marcia smiled at her and Brad sensed that the ladies might eventually get along with each other. "How's it going?"

"Well, maybe you two should come in." She said.

They followed her in, to see Aunt Jane standing in the aisle, wearing a red and black lace teddy.

"Well, my dears...what do you think?" She asked them.

"Hi, Aunt Jane." Brad smiled and nodded and turned to Mary.

"Why don't you give Charlie and Cyndi a call."

"Okay." Mary said, following them as they walked toward the door. "First you, then Charlie...my gosh all the men in this town are getting married."

"Are we getting married?" Brad asked Marcia as they continued up the street. Marcia took his hand and squeezed it. As they approached the pizzeria, Tim was just opening the door.

"Hey Brad, how are you."

"Fine." He answered. "I hear that you're the new manager. How do you like it?"

"Well, I can see why you stayed on the job as long as you did." Tim couldn't help but smile, and Brad knew that for once he had hired the right man for the job.

"Great." Brad patted him on the shoulder, then they started making their way back up the street. "Good luck."

Walking up Main Street, Brad felt that every thought that had been rolling around in his head was settling into place. He knew that he would spend his entire life in the North Woods and that Marcia and he would indeed live happily ever after. They would live in their home in the tree and they would continue to write and publish their books.

And perhaps, for inspiration, they would have other adventures.

About the Author

Originally from the North Woods, Kevin Virgil Wallace currently lives in Los Angeles. He is the author of the three books which make up the *Ordinary Project; Ordinary Guy, Ordinary Vacation* and *Ordinary Redemption*. He has also co-authored two non-fiction books, *Contemporary Turned Wood: New Perspectives in a Rich Tradition* and *Baskets: Tradition and Beyond*.

Printed in the United States
3949